I0675670

Odinochka:
Armenian Tales from the Gulag

Odinochka:
Armenian Tales from the Gulag

Suren Oganessian

Vishapakar Publishing

Saint Petersburg, Florida. 2016

Copyright © 2016 by Suren Oganessian

All rights reserved. This book or any portion thereof may not be reproduced or used in any manner whatsoever without the express written permission of the publisher except for the use of brief quotations in a book review or scholarly journal.

First Printing: 2016

ISBN <978-0-9974494-0-2>

Vishapakar Publishing
5447 Haines Rd. #173
St. Petersburg, FL 33714

http://surenoganessian.webs.com/

To my grandfather, Suren Oganessian the First; if he hadn't taken an opportunity one stormy Siberian night and escaped the Gulag, you would not be reading this.

Gulag

In the early morning blackness, we filter out of our wooden bunkers and into the stinging cold. It's shortly before the morning roll call. Someone shimmies up a pole, and reaches for the thermostat on the side of the building where the cold winds can't tamper with its accuracy, brushing off the frost with a gloved hand. It is half past five; daylight won't come for another three hours or so, because it's winter. Daylight is fleeting now, and is getting shorter by the day. The Siberian coldness attacks every extremity, something the meager coat, undershirt and earflap hat of our winter uniforms are ill-equipped to completely shield us from. Surely today it is too cold to work. It certainly feels like -40 degrees. When it gets that cold there is really little difference between -20 and -40, so it was hard to tell for sure. If it was more than -40 Celsius, we'd be allowed to stay in our bunkers and wait out the cold. I haven't seen this happen yet, but then again this is my first winter here.

"Minus twenty-seven." the Russian prisoner calls out, a man named Boris, before sliding to the ground again.

The small crowd groans and grumbles, cheated by Mother Nature once again. While this information is relayed in several different languages among the crowd, Boris insists to Russian-speaking members of his work team that he didn't breathe on the thermometer at all, but accusations were still hurled at him. I look down at the snowy ground and shiver, breathing deep ragged breaths through congested lungs and trying to avoid another coughing fit, watching my white breath puff in the air like smoke as I exhaled. At this temperature it hurts to breathe; having one's lungs filled with such cold air is not pleasant even to a healthy prisoner. I am almost certain that I am running a fever. If a doctor deems me too sick to work I could still get the day off, but it would take a lot of convincing.

"So then, Bard, it'll be your turn laying the bricks today. You wheeled the mortar up yesterday," comes the voice of Narek, another member of my work team, the one that the guards had put in charge of us by way of seniority.

Bard is my nickname, given to me by the other prisoners because I am always telling stories either during work or before bed; my actual birth name is Vartan Manukyan.

"Yes, I remember." I answer, my voice weak until I clear my throat, and spit out the mucous.

Brick-laying is a hard job; at least when you wheel the mortar up you get to be near the furnace which served to keep the mortar from freezing. One could stop to warm their hands if no one was watching. That was the second best job someone could get on this project, the best and warmest being mixing the mortar, which our team isn't in charge of.

"Good, no arguments this time," Narek insists, while adjusting the bandage he always kept wrapped around his left eye.

"It was Viken that was arguing last time," I protest, feeling an itch in my chest as I raise my voice.

"You should learn not to provoke him," Narek says, before I finally succumb to a coughing fit, "You alright? Are you sick?"

I breathe heavily to stave off the coughs, and nod.

"Lucky bastard. You might just be sick enough to make the list. After breakfast, go get yourself looked at. But for our team's sake I hope you can work."

A whistle blows loudly.

"Attention!" a Russian guard calls out.

We all march toward the front of the camp, before the barbed-wire gates. They then perform a roll call, calling out our numbers. I am Prisoner C421; the number is on my hat and on the back of my coat, painted on a rectangular patch of white cloth sewn onto my uniform. Then the soldiers pat us down, making sure we aren't smuggling a shiv, some extra food, or wearing any extra clothes. Those caught sneaking another shirt or jacket on beneath their uniform to keep warm would have to strip their clothes off in the morning cold. If the captain was in a particularly foul mood that morning, that prisoner could be sent to odinochka, or solitary confinement. A prison within a prison. Slang terms varied on odinochka, but the most common was 'the hole', or "the cooler". The guards didn't need much of a reason to put a prisoner in these cells, but you normally wouldn't be thrown in until the end of the day, so they could still get a full day's work out of you. I have seen prisoners be put in there for having neglected to get the number repainted on their hat. I myself had never tried sneaking an extra layer of clothes on or smuggling any extra portions of food in my coat; in the last seven months I'd worked hard to keep myself low-key, and managed to slip under the guards' radar. I wasn't one of the favorites for the guards to harass. Being caught smuggling anything like an improvised knife would be trouble I didn't need.

After we're frisked, the guards line us up and march us to the mess hall. In winter we are rationed 100 grams of baked bread to last us throughout the day and some water, and we are given a bowl of goulash for every meal (consisting of little more than warmed up water with bits of cabbage, and occasionally scraps of fish). In the summer it was only the bread and water. Sometimes, not even bread. So in a way, winter was both the best time and the worst time to be in a Siberian Gulag. The catch was that your team had to meet a work quota. If you didn't get a certain amount of work done by the end of the day, your team went without food. The guards devised this system so they wouldn't have to do as much work. We were motivated to do our slave labor by each other rather than a guard barking orders at us while we worked. If someone wasn't pulling their own weight and cost the team a meal, it was a simple matter to orchestrate an "accident" on the job, or get them thrown in the hole for something they didn't do. The fact that no one had done it to Viken yet probably had more to do with how good a worker he was than anybody actually liking him; though he has certainly been pushing his luck in that area, with his attitude.

Our team always ate together at a long wooden table crammed with other prisoners. There were five of us, all Armenians. Though the majority of the prisoners were Ukrainian, Latvian or Jewish, there were still several other languages spoken at the camp, so we were divided by language so we could understand one another. Every one of us had a story. Indeed, everyone in the camp had stories, which all had the same tragic end. Whilst working or resting in our bunks I'd managed to learn the stories of those in my team who I could converse with freely in Armenian without the Russian-speaking guards overhearing us.

Prisoner C322

Narek is our foreman; a tall, strong young man in his mid-twenties. He looks like he was probably quite handsome too, before getting those scars on his face and losing an eye. His nose is slightly crooked, as if it had been broken and hadn't healed properly. He's been at this camp longer than me, but as soon as we met and I got a look at his face, I at once tried to coax his story out of him. He resisted for a long time, by either changing the subject or outright refusing to discuss it, until a night last summer, as we lay in our bunk beds. On a whim I asked him what part of Armenia he was from, hoping to get him to tell me about his past from this starting point. As Narek told it, he was born around the city of Kars, at the time near the eastern-most boundary of the Ottoman Empire. Most of us at the camps, when pressed, referred to the biggest city near the village we actually came from as our hometown. From what little he told me, his family fled east to the relative safety of Russian Armenia, after the Turks came for the Armenians during the war.

There was one part of his past Narek mentioned often, even without my pressing him. He claimed, beaming with pride each time he said it, that his father was among the soldiers that defeated the invading Turks at Sardarapat in 1918.

"Without people like my father there'd be no Armenia," he'd say.

Of course, after the Soviets took control, Armenia barely existed anyway. Stalin saw to that. Showing pride in one's country was something that landed a person here in the camps. Narek was one of those strong Armenian nationalists who longed for a day when Armenia would be independent again, the kinds of people

Stalin was trying to wipe out. I suppose I was one of these people too, before my arrest. Now I was just trying to live.

The night I got him to speak to me though, he went further with his story. In the late 1920's he became an organizer of the underground Armenian Revolutionary Federation, a Dashnak as they were called. They were the party that ruled Armenia during its two year stint of independence. He even claimed to be a good friend of their former leader Garegin Nzhdeh. I thought he was making that up. Of course he wouldn't believe that I'd met Aram Manukyan back in Van either. Anyway this was just the organization for people like him; their goal first and foremost was Armenia's independence, just as it had been during the Ottoman years. Little wonder the party was outlawed. I myself had been arrested for being part of this group, though I was only a member, not an organizer. Organizers would try and recruit new members to their cause, usually by handing out pamphlets in back alleys that they'd printed in secret and hoping the Cheka didn't catch them.

No one at the camp had been able to extract his full name or how he'd been arrested, but it was an open secret that his permanent eye injury, as well as his scars and dislocated nose, came during an interrogation. Taking his past as a Dashnak organizer into consideration and what I've heard happens to people in that position if they get arrested, I can deduce that the soldiers had probably tried to force him to reveal the names of other ARF members. Perhaps in his steadfast pride, he refused, and was punished thusly until either he finally spoke, or the guards tired of beating him. I can't say for sure if he ever gave in. As was common practice, after the torture session he'd been forced to sign a waiver and agree to never speak of what had happened in there, with the fear of death upon him. This was the real reason he was quiet about his past. And if the interrogators were successful in getting the information from him, his guilt prevented him from ever telling anyone what had happened in the interrogation room too. Since that day he had been one of the most obedient of prisoners. But, they were never able to beat all of his pride out of him.

Prisoner E456

Sitting next to me at the table was Avedik Khanigian, a man of medium stature with dark skin and a short black beard. His story was one of the most interesting. I remember the day he was unloaded from the train with a new group of prisoners transferred from Madekh, a prison in Georgia. It was September and the days were warmer. As our group toiled at the lumber yards five miles from camp a soldier escorted him toward us and announced he'd be joining our work group because he was Armenian. Armenians were grouped together to overcome the language barrier, but this didn't help Avedik much at first. As it turned out, he hadn't spoken much Armenian since adolescence. What little he did speak was Western Armenian with a mixture of Turkish, and some of us had trouble understanding him. It was a dialect spoken only in what's now Turkey and wherever Armenians from there had migrated. He and I became quick allies because I'm from Van, a city around the same area, and could therefore translate when the others misunderstood him. But some in our group, most notably Viken and Narek, disliked him at first and viewed him as little more than a would-be Kurd who had betrayed his Armenian heritage.

According to Avedik, his family had been spared deportation during the war by remaining hidden among kindly Kurdish neighbors, though to remain safe they needed to integrate and adopt the Kurdish lifestyle, becoming Muslims. As the 1920's wore on the Kurds proved not to be quite the model minority the Turks had hoped for, after disposing of its other "unruly" minorities. The Ararat province, peopled by Kurds and a few leftover Islamic Armenians who both had reason to be disdained at Turkey's rule, broke away and declared independence. Avedik rose to high ranks among the rebel groups, fighting for the Kurdish cause.

The Soviet authorities, under the pretext of discussing aid and weapons for the Kurds in their revolt, invited him to Armenia. No sooner than he set foot on Soviet soil, he was arrested. He was first sent to Yerevan, then to Madekh, and finally to Siberia, with a five year sentence. Even though he was not a Soviet citizen, he'd been placed in a Gulag, a victim of the USSR's attempts to woo Turkey toward communism. Maybe they'd changed their minds about aiding the rebellion at the last minute, or maybe Soviet and Turkish authorities had been plotting the capture of Avedik behind the scenes all along. No one knew what would happen to him after the five year sentence was up. Maybe they would find a way to keep him longer, or he wasn't expected to even make it in the Gulag that long. I found him to be a respectable man, though, and as much a victim of both Turkey and the Soviet Union as any of us.

Prisoner A579

Krikor Der Bayrakdarian had been a priest of the Armenian Apostolic Church before the Soviet Union absorbed Armenia into its borders. He always lived in the Russian portion of Armenia, probably sparing him from the sword of the Turk. But, when religion in Stalin's Russia was outlawed, the churches in Armenia were either abandoned or relegated into museums. Krikor's faith was too strong to be stopped by this, and he held sermons in secret in the basement of his home. This was not to last; Soviet spies were able to infiltrate one of his masses and apprehend him, sending him to prison. He kept his faith even in this frozen hell, often praying silently before meals and in his bunk before going to sleep. He became the conscience of our group in many ways. On occasion he would seek someone to join him in prayer, or give us biblical advice, but this often fell on deaf ears here. Very few of us had fully kept our faith by this stage of our imprisonment. Josef Stalin, whose smug grin stared down on us from portraits on the walls wherever we turned, was God here. And he was a jealous, vengeful deity.

Despite religious differences Krikor was accepting of Avedik when he first entered the group. He did however offer to convert Avedik back to the religion of his ancestors. Having lost everything meaningful to him, and fully expecting to die either in the Gulag or when he ever got out, Avedik was fast becoming an agnostic. The work schedule here left little time to pray facing Mecca five times a day anyway. Krikor's attempts to parlay this waning faith in Allah into a conversion to Christianity haven't worked yet, but watching him try I have to admit Krikor is quite dedicated. Viken, for reasons I'll explain, is a tougher case, having been a staunch atheist at least since his incarceration if not earlier. He balked at Krikor's notion of a God, and said that if there were one He must be conveniently overlooking Siberia. And the Armenians for the last forty years or so for that matter. The rest of us in the group mainly fell somewhere in between these two rigid points of view; blind faith and atheism. I already became agnostic long before setting foot in the camps. Could a God justify the things I've seen in my lifetime?

Prisoner A837

Viken Koshanetyan's tale may have been the worst of all, at least as far as our team went. Viken was never the most talkative among us unless he was throwing an insult or complaining on the job. But I remember well the day he finally opened up to us. It was a rare moment that hasn't repeated itself since. It was after the lights had been turned out at our bunks, Narek and I had been dwelling on the current state of Armenia; something as I've said Narek was always passionate about. Nobody was here for thinking that Armenia was better off under Soviet rule of course, but I pondered whether or not Armenia being annexed was the only thing keeping it from being wiped off the map completely. Narek contended that Sardarapat had been a lesson to the Turks that they could never fully extinguish us. Viken, overhearing our banter, scoffed at us both, dismissing us as 'imbecilic Dashnaks with a pipe dream' before, in excruciating detail, telling us exactly why Armenian nationalists had been a bane to his existence.

Viken had thought like us once. He'd been a history teacher at Sev Kar before his imprisonment, and a member of the Communist Party. But eventually he was dismissed for harboring nationalistic tendencies. The authorities didn't agree with the way he taught the history of Armenia in his classes. It was illegal to show any kind of national pride. It was also illegal to speak openly about what had happened to the Armenians in Turkey during the Great War, something Viken was very opinionated about. Eventually he was arrested for supposedly being a member of the Armenian Revolutionary Federation, an assertion he denied. He was taken to Madekh. In prison the Bolsheviks wanted him to expose other members of the Dashnak and give them information on the organization, but he knew no names, nor anything else about it.

In a futile effort to try and get Viken to talk, Stalin's secret police tortured him by having him stand in a bucket of freezing water outside overnight, depriving him of sleep. On his left hand three of his fingertips were missing, severed during interrogations. When nothing worked, one night they took him outside, gave him a shovel, and forced him to dig his own grave. Once finished, he was given five minutes to confess to being a Dashnak before they would shoot him. When he said nothing, they blindfolded him, and lowered him into the grave. The interrogator gave him one more chance to confess before being shot.

Viken coldly replied, "Just shoot me."

At this, the interrogator gave up and returned him to his cell, where later he was forced to sign a waiver like Narek's. The next day, Viken was loaded onto a train, and transferred to Siberia. Unlike Narek, however, the waiver hadn't scared him from telling us what had happened. He'd already seen the worst that they could do, nothing scared him now.

These events had left Viken a bitter, angry man, very hard to get along with. Only the guards were exempt from his rage, because he knew only too well what they could do to him. And he especially hated Narek and me. He may have been a nationalist once, but not anymore. The camps had broken him, beaten and tortured the Armenian out of him. Although I felt compassion for the man after he related to us his story, I knew he was no friend of mine. He had no friends, nor did he want any. The only thing that motivated him into cooperating with us at all when we were put to work was that if he didn't, he wouldn't be fed. Though I had to wonder how much of a will to live a man like him could have, who according to his story was so calm staring into the face of death, even beckoning it.

Gulag

I eat my soup from a cheap tin pot, not wasting a drop, soaking my bread in it to make the bread less coarse. The hot soup feels wonderful on my throat, which is sore and raw from coughing. The soup may be bland, thin and tasteless, but this is perhaps the only part of the day I ever enjoy, besides going to my bunk for sleep. I also eat with my prized possession - a tin spoon. Spoons were a luxury in the camps. Having burned my lips on the pot one too many times, one day last summer I resolved to trade my bread to a starving prisoner who'd made a spoon for themselves in the camp workshop. I went hungry that day, but in the months since I've not regretted the transaction. But you have to eat quickly, and you have to keep an eye on your food. I learned never to let go of my bread during any part of the meal. It would be snatched by someone else the moment you looked away.

I'll confess to having swiped loaves of bread from hapless newcomers who didn't know how the camps worked a few times myself. I am not proud of some of the things I have had to do to stay alive here. But in such an environment as this, one has to look out for themselves. Someone dies from starvation or malnutrition every day in these camps. It's a horrid way to go out; your body has nothing to eat so it begins to eat itself. My own body has been eating itself since coming here. Hunger is a constant companion. I can see all of my ribs now. Of course under these circumstances you're going to steal food if you have the slightest chance to do so. And when someone collapses from exhaustion while laboring or marching long distances in the snow, you want to be the first to steal his coat, his boots, his pants, his rations, his spoon, as he screams and begs for mercy. They'll do everything but cannibalize you if you collapse. The guards don't care. Once someone can no longer work they're of no use anyway. But they still don't want you wearing layers because you could be smuggling something, so they might take the jacket away after you steal it.

If you're sick they allow you to stay in your bunk, at the cost of some of your rations, but their definition of too sick to work is very specific. Today might be my lucky day. Then again I haven't been able to get a day off that wasn't because of a heavy blizzard since arriving in the spring, despite having come down with a fever back in August too. It was very easy for someone to work themselves to death on account of sickness, starvation and malnutrition, not to mention the risks of hypothermia and frostbite. Before winter turned the place into barren snow dunes I would occasionally supplement my meager diet with grass and bugs, anything remotely edible I could find while laboring. It was something I'd learned to do back in 1915. These days, the snow provided some extra water so I could avoid dehydration, but that was it. Eating snow had its own risks too at any rate, because it cost precious body heat, so it was a last resort.

After our allotted twenty minutes for breakfast, a whistle blows, and we are marched outside into the bitter cold again. Now is the time. I approach one of the guards, forcing myself into a coughing fit to make it obvious that my symptoms are not being faked.

Infirmary

"Prisoner C421 is complaining about some sort of chest congestion," the guard explains to the nurse, "See if he's in any condition to work."

The infirmary is little more than a wooden shack, filled with rows of beds of ailing, groaning prisoners, the smells of dying flesh, but it is heated by a furnace. It is the warmest building I'd been inside in quite a while (because even the dining hall, packed with so many people, manages to maintain a certain chill in the air). It is run by a single nurse and doctor, both male and Russian. Having picked up some Russian myself since moving east fifteen years ago, I can keep up with their conversation. I'm seated onto an examination table as the doctor removes my coat and undershirt.

"I want you to take deep breaths for me," says the doctor.

He places the metal stethoscope to my chest. It feels like an ice cube, and I flinch. But soon, I take as deep a breath as I can muster without erupting into another coughing fit. My breaths are labored and ragged. The doctor asks me to do this several more times, before checking the inside of my mouth. I stare off at the dying prisoners as the doctor makes his assessment. I've always hated hospitals. I worked at one briefly as a child; forcibly volunteered is a better term. Out of the corner of my eye I almost think I a pair of bloody nails and a horseshoe, lying on a steel tray. It's just my imagination, a ghost from my past come to haunt me; the nails are only scalpels.

"I think he may be developing bronchitis," the doctor says.

"Is this serious?" demands the Russian guard, "He is to be laboring on the new barracks today. We need as much manpower as we can get if it is to be ready for the new inmates as scheduled."

"If it goes untreated, it could go from being bronchitis to pneumonia," the doctor warns.

"But it isn't bronchitis or pneumonia yet," the guard said, stating it rather than posing it as a question.

I sit on the examination table, waiting for my fate to be determined.

"No, not yet," the doctor concedes.

"We'll get one more day of work out of you," the guard says to me with a wry grin, "You can get pneumonia later."

Gulag

It is time to get to work. We are building a new structure for the camp. It will be another barrack to relieve the overcrowding problem the camp is beginning to have. These days Stalin sees enemies left and right, and we need more room to house them all. Not enough prisoners are dying to make room for new ones. Around two months ago they extended the tall barbed wire fences that surrounded the camp around an empty area where we were erecting the two-story structure, which would be built of wood and brick. The lucky thing about this assignment was that we didn't need to be marched outside the camp to do it. We were close to the Mess Hall and our barracks. This did however mean that we would need to work the entire time, because the guards would be eyeing us like hawks. This summer our team had been assigned to pave a road five kilometers outside the camp. We walked the whole way. Summers in Siberia are comparatively comfortable, but having to march that far in the winter would be entirely different. The good in this case outweighed the bad.

The snow crunches beneath my boots as the guard escorts me from the infirmary to the work area in almost total darkness. Three teams were assigned this task, ours and teams of Latvians and Tartars. Snow had piled up around the structure overnight; our first task is to dig the snow away with shovels, which is already being done. The guard picks a shovel up from the ground as we near the building and forces it into my hands, before trudging off. The work area is lit by gas lanterns, and I use those to try and find my team. I find the four of them clearing snow from around the entrance, and join them.

"Make room, here comes Vartan," said Avedik, as I take a spot between him and Krikor, and began shoveling snow away from the wall.

"They're making you work anyway, are they?" Krikor asks in a low voice.

I nod.

"God be with you," he whispers, "Let me know if I can help you."

"I'll be alright," I say, though I probably won't be.

"Well you'd best be," says Viken, digging beside Krikor, "Your case of the sniffles better not cost me dinner."

A guard strikes Viken in the arm with the butt of his rifle and shouts at him to stop talking. Other guards shout orders and encourage us to hurry so that we could get to laying bricks. No one usually speaks as we dig, with the guards watching over our shoulders, we simply do as we were told. There's a danger to working too hard in this cold; if you work up a sweat, the sweat could freeze and you could be hypothermic in a short time. But the guards don't worry about things like that; this building is proof enough that we are quite replaceable.

I asked Narek once what it must be like to go out freezing to death of hypothermia. He said the shivering was the hard part, and the part that lasted the longest. Soon you lose feeling in your hands and feet, and you can't move them anymore. Your mind starts to wander and you might start seeing things that aren't there or mumbling to yourself without realizing it. Once you stop shivering you go numb, and the rest is easy, peaceful, like falling asleep. You just give in and let the coldness take you, except at that point you don't even feel the cold anymore. I asked him how he knew that; he confessed that's just the way he imagined it being like, after watching it happen to others. I imagine he's probably right. It wouldn't be such a bad way to go out. It sounds better than starving, or being shot. Or any of the thousands of other ways you could die in a Gulag.

And as I dig I am already beginning to feel faint. Maybe not enough air is making it through my clogged lungs. After around three quarters of an hour, our digging is finished, and we are able to continue the construction. It's still dark out, but the starry sky is giving way to the gradual brightening of dawn. Krikor, Narek and I go up the ramp to the top floor, still without a roof and exposed to open air. There is a pile of red bricks waiting to be laid. We wait a few moments for the mortar to be mixed and heated down below. Waiting and standing still is actually worse than laying bricks. If you're not moving, the coldness becomes all that you can occupy your mind with. I now long for the job I'd had yesterday, being near the furnace and the warm mortar. In due time, Viken arrives up the ramp with a wheel barrel of steaming hot mortar.

"Hurry it up," he orders as I use a hand shovel to spread the mortar onto the unfinished wall and lay a brick atop, then spreading the steaming mortar over the top and the sides of the brick. If I could squish the mortar between my fingers to warm my hands I would. But it is far too hot.

We need to work fast; the team that lays the least bricks will miss out on supper. Luckily I'd gotten good at it; I still remember laying bricks back in Van to fortify buildings during the war. Viken stirs the mortar with a steel rod, because as hot as it is it still doesn't take long for it to cool and harden in these temperatures if you let it sit without stirring. So, for the next few hours, this is what we do. The sun slowly rises, not offering much warmth. When we started the brick wall was as high as my knee, by half past eleven it is as high as my hips. My hands are raw from laying so many bricks. Each worked on a different wall, and we are working at nearly the same speed. But we all knew we were participating in a sick game for the sake of the amusement of our guards. The loser would get no dinner.

At noon the whistle for lunch blows, and the guards call us down and marches us single file to the mess hall. Only those present at the camp, which hadn't been marched off into the tundra for heavy labor, are in attendance, so it is less crowded and chaotic than usual. We receive more gruel, and a cup of water. As we line up to the counter, Viken, in line ahead of me, slyly reaches over with his pot and places it against my hand as I hold a tray, scalding it and causing me to wince and drop my own pot on the counter, spilling some of my precious soup. I give him a dirty look, blowing on my hand, but he looks away as if nothing had happened. This is typical behavior from him. It was better not to say anything. But I'm getting tired of taking his constant hazing.

Our bread rations given to us at breakfast have to last all day. I've been keeping mine in the inside pocket of my coat. I try to savor it at lunch and only have a few bites so there will be plenty left at dinner, after a long day of work. I watch as Avedik makes a go for Viken's bread, making like he's reaching for his cup but going a little further. Viken catches this and grabs Avedik's wrist, as tightly as he could with the missing fingertips on his left hand. Avedik pulls away, nursing his wrist and scowling before turning his attention back to his meager soup.

"I think we're going to beat the other teams today," Narek says to me quietly, making small talk as we eat.

This was discouraged by the guards, but we often whispered to one another while eating.

"Yeah, the tartars are moving like frozen mud," I reply, "I think we'll finish a whole wall by dinner."

In a moment of thoughtlessness, I place my bread down and began scooping goulash into my mouth with my spoon. And after a few moments, when I reach for my bread I find that it had been taken.

I look around the table for a guilty face, "Who took my bread?"

My team was silent for a few moments, until Krikor, the most honest among us, speaks up, "Viken took it. He's been stalking your meal like a vulture this entire time."

I turn to Viken, who was sitting diagonally from me across the table.

"Give me my bread back."

He takes it from inside his coat, mockingly dipping it into his soup and taking a savory bite, "You looked like you were done with it."

"I told you to give it back!"

"I think I've earned it. It's Dashnaks like you that got me where I am now," he says, gorging himself on the bread roll.

There's nothing I can really do about it without making a scene.

"I will give you half of my bread if you like, Manukyan," Krikor offers.

"No thanks, that won't be necessary," I decline, "You're here for practicing religion. Apparently entitlement to food around here depends on why you were arrested now."

"Viken, why don't you give Vartan your other bread?" Narek asks, as irritated as I was with Viken's attitude.

"Because I deserve it." Viken says, "I shouldn't have to listen to you just because you got picked as our leader, one-eye. Goddamn Dashnak."

"Shut up you guys," Avedik warns, "If a guard hears us bickering we'll probably lose out on dinner."

"Avedik, the savior of the Kurds, you're really no different from these two little 'rebels' here. People like you are the reason these prisons exist. Just like the Dashnak are the ones who caused the Turks to remove us all from our homeland."

"That's not true at all," I protest.

"Struck a nerve have I, Bard?" Viken mocks, "You're from Van, che? You were part of that rebellion when you were a child, weren't you? I've heard you say so a couple times. "

"That's enough Viken," says Avedik. "You're talking like a Turk."

My eyes narrow, as I try my best to keep my anger in check.

"You should know all about this," he continues, ignoring Avedik as he dips my bread into his soup again, "Revolutionaries, they're all the same, stirring the pot until it backfires on all of us. If people like you would just shut your mouths and deal with the way things are instead of going against the system all the time, you would still be living in Turkey peacefully, and I would still have all my fingers, and Narek would have two eyes, and Siberia would just be someplace we learned about in school, a spot on the map and nothing more. Don't you get it? It was all your own fault, and the rest of the innocents who never cared whether Armenia was independent or not have had to pay with their blood for your idiotic aspirations."

In his face I see the eyes of Jevdet Bey and Josef Stalin all at once staring back at me. His words echo every villain who'd made my life hell for the last fifteen years. Fed up with listening to Viken blame me for everything that had gone wrong in my life, I lunge across the table at him with the only thing I could use as a weapon; my spoon. Trays crash to the floor as several other prisoners stand up to watch. The two of us fall back to the floor with me on top. As he struggles to push me away I manage to jab the spoon into his temples a few times until he grabs my wrist. I swear to him that I'm going to scoop his fucking eyes out with that spoon.

A guard blows his whistle and soon several of them swarm us, pulling us apart. Rage overtakes me. I struggle against their grip but my fists have been subdued. Another prisoner at the next table takes this chance to steal food for himself while the others in his team were preoccupied, until he is caught, and another fight breaks out between them. And then two more fights break out elsewhere in the room. It's a chain reaction. The Mess Hall soon becomes a war zone, punches are thrown, and spoons, trays and plates are used as weapons. Whistles pierce the air, and the guards evacuate the room, leaving me to try and hunt Viken down through the crowd, but he crawled away.

Within moments, the doors to the Mess Hall open again, and guards hurl several steel canisters into the room. When they hit the ground, they explode with tear gas. Rioters panic and disperse. Some continue to fight, but the gas fills our lungs, making us cough, gag, and fall to the ground. I am especially hard hit by this; I fall to my knees, coughing and gagging until I see spots and flashes before my eyes. I am suffocating. The room is then flooded by soldiers in gas masks, dragging us out of the room and into the snow. A few who struggled to fight back against the guards were shot in the head and tossed aside. When they come for me I go limp and am roughly dragged into the snow.

"That's the one who started it," a guard says to another.

It's the one who'd subdued me before they evacuated the Mess Hall. The other guard nods and they pick me up by the arms. All I can do is cough and hack because of the gas. The guard strikes me in the head with his club. I see even more flashes before my eyes.

"This is the sick one, C421. I doubt we'll be getting any more work out of him today."

"Then we send him straight to odinochka now instead of waiting for tonight," the guard says, before stooping down to look me in the eye, "You hear me, dog? *Three nights in odinochka!* And if you live through that, you'll be sent to the Disciplinary Camp."

He slaps me across the face. I receive my death sentence.

The guards seize me at gunpoint, and drag me to odinochka, what we called 'the hole', solitary confinement. It is a row of cells made of stone, with barred windows that opened into the frozen tundra air. At any given time there could be as many as twelve prisoners, one in each cell. The room is lit by a single light bulb, flickering on the ceiling. The prisoners who'd been shot in the head for resisting were luckier than I. My coughing and gagging is uncontrollable as they drag me through the snow, without much effort after how thin I've become over the past months. The guards throw me into the dank prison. I land on my knees against the cement floor and cry out in pain, clutching my right kneecap, which took the worst of it. As soon as I hear death's door close behind me, I know that this is it.

Surviving one night in here would be an achievement, but three? I doubt that I would even survive until morning. Then would come the Disciplinary Camp. I've heard tales about these camps. If it's possible to be worse than a Gulag, these camps are. They'll torture you to death there. It's a death camp.

There is a wooden cot in the room, hard and uncomfortable. No blanket or mattress. Just wooden planks. Perhaps the blankets used to be there, but got ruined somehow, and the guards had neglected to replace them. Or perhaps they never meant this 'odinochka' to be comfortable; the more likely scenario. It was hardly any softer than the stone ground. I drag my body toward the cot and sit down on it, rubbing my wounds. I feel a bump on my head already, and I can hardly move my legs. I don't think they're broken, but they hurt. Groaning in pain I stare up at the light bulb, illuminating this dim, lonely room.

My time on Earth has been full of hardship and pain, pain that I keep inside, that I never let anyone see. If now is my time to die, after all I had been through, losing my family, the Siege of Van, the war with the Turks, I actually don't mind so much. I have been through enough hardship for twenty lives, and I'm not even thirty years old yet. All my life I have just wanted to escape this world. Stories were my only means of escape, until now. Now I am going to make the final escape. But my one and only regret in life is never telling anyone my own story. For when I die, my memories, and all those who now exist only within them, will die with me.

Vartan Manukyan

My name is Vartan Manukyan. I was born in a small village of Ardamet in the Van Villayet on April 17, 1902. I'm quite sure this village probably has a Turkish or Kurdish name by now. But I wouldn't know. I haven't been there in about sixteen years. Not since being moved to the orphanage. And looking at maps is too painful for me now. It's painful for any Armenian. I can't say I remember my past with complete clarity. Some memories get jumbled with others and contradict one another, or I convince myself that it happened one way when it really may not have, or a memory might be so painful that I've suppressed it. And I suppose, by telling other people's stories instead of my own, by becoming the narrator of the world around me, I've been trying to escape my own story. My eyes see everything in the world but themselves. There's nothing unusual about that. My memory might be a bit hazy but there are moments and people who stand out, that live and breathe in my memory to this day. Memories I can't get rid of, despite my best efforts.

I suppose what makes my tale of woe a little different from the other Armenians at this prison is that my family had already crumbled away by 1915. I was an orphan even before the great calamity struck us down, before death grew strong and swallowed us. My mother came down with typhus fever in 1909 and died, along with my older sister Sosie, a girl of whom I only have the faintest glimmers of a memory. Typhus was very widespread in those days. It was the only thing that was killing everyone regardless of race or religion. At least those victimized by the epidemic were spared the scimitar later. My father and I helped each other through the grief. His name was Mher Manukyan, and was a teacher at an all-boys school. Often I would have to come with him to the schoolhouse because there was nobody else to watch me. I learned to sit and be quiet and obedient, but while doing so I absorbed everything he taught. He taught me on his own time too, about how to read and write, about history. He would tell me stories too, old Armenian folktales and epics that he learned from his father, and that would be passed around and rehearsed in Armenian villages in the winter. Back home he had shelves of old books that I'd indulge in. Stories like Davit of Sasun, Ara the Handsome; those were my favorites growing up. I've carried that with me to the present. In all, my father was a very sad man, but loving nonetheless, and a good parent. I still think of him sometimes.

I lost him in the autumn of 1914. He was drafted into the Turkish army to fight the Russians, and almost assuredly killed. Armenian soldiers in the Ottoman army didn't often survive long; on the battlefield the enemy was both in front of them and behind them. I only assume he was killed because after the war I never heard from him again. When he was drafted, I stayed with neighbors for two months, awaiting a reply to my letters, before it became clear to them that he wasn't ever going to reply. I held steadfast onto the hope that the war was going to end and my father was going to come get me. But they wouldn't wait for that. They couldn't support another mouth to feed, so decided to bring me to an orphanage in nearby Van, situated within the walled portion of the city known as Aigestan to the locals. There were a few orphanages in Van, the biggest being the one run by Dr. and Mrs. Raynolds, missionaries from America. That one housed somewhere around four hundred Armenian orphans. I was going to a smaller orphanage, run by a German couple, also missionaries. In an odd way, being in Van is probably what saved my life in the end.

The Orphanage at Van

Van was a beautiful garden-like place, surrounded by large mountains and a vast azure lake that also bore its name. Every house had a vineyard, and at its center the city was dominated by Castle Rock, a rocky outcropping containing an ancient fort from the empire of Urartu, a reminder from another age, its stone towers a silent witness to the triumph and turmoil of centuries raging below. From those towers I was but a speck being escorted through the gate in the walls, but it greeted me the same way it greeted all who entered its domain; kings, sultans, peasants alike. The streets bustled with commotion, full of life. Wagons pulled by horses or donkeys dominated the stony streets, and the city stank of them. Automobiles were nearly unheard of, a luxury of the west. Stands run by charismatic salesmen selling fruit, wine, jars of honey or jewelry made their presence known along the sides of the streets, which were lined by wood plank sidewalks. The big city was quite a shock for a villager like me, so unaccustomed to the noise and the crowds, so many buildings and people all in one place.

It was when I saw the Armenian orphanage, a dark, slightly dilapidated two-story building of stone and mortar that rose from the ground like a large gray tombstone, that I had to face the fact that I was alone in this world. There's no lonelier a feeling than being the new kid at an orphanage. I didn't think I belonged here. My father was alive. He was fighting the Russians. I wasn't an orphan. I couldn't be.

The couple who'd taken me in did no more than drop me off and fill out some forms, and they were gone. I was immediately escorted down a hallway by one of the nursemaids, a tall woman with jet-black hair and a white dress, stopping at a door where the first sounds I remember hearing were that of a young girl sobbing her heart out behind it.

"No, no you're making me ugly!" she shrieked.

"Sit down, young lady!' an adult woman scolded, "We can't have the children at this orphanage infested with lice!"

"I do not have lice!"

"You will if we don't cut that hair."

"But I'm going to look like a boy!"

"You can wear a headscarf," the woman insisted, "Now sit still."

The nurse opened the door, and ushered me in.

"We have another new one today," said the nurse to the one doing the hair cutting.

It was a bathroom, with a tin bathtub at one end and the girl seated on a chair in the middle as an older woman cut her hair, which looked to have gone down to the small of the girl's back. The girl turned to look at me, with a gasp.

"Don't bring someone else in here to watch!"
"Young girl you're being most unruly. We have rules to abide by at this orphanage you know, and so far you've been breaking all of them."

The girl sniffled and remained silent as she lost her dark-colored locks bit by bit. Her hair was gone in a few minutes. Never having seen a bald girl before, I remained quiet, pretending to look the other way when she looked at me, but staring at her when she was turned away.

Once finished, the nurse shooed the girl out. She looked back at me one more time as she left the room with wet eyes; her eyes met mine and at once I knew we both understood the pain in one another's eyes.

My straight black hair fell nearly to my shoulders and threatened to start covering my eyes, having not received cutting in months. Within a few minutes though, I was bald. I didn't mind it so much, not like a girl would. If it would keep me from getting lice, all the better. But it was okay for a boy to be bald. I couldn't help feeling sorry for the girl who'd just been here.

"Alright young man, the rest of the children are having their mathematics lessons now, we can send you right in," said the nurse who'd escorted me here.

"Mathematics?" I asked.

For some reason or another I'd gotten the idea that they didn't have a school at orphanages. I hadn't been in school since the war started. I doubted very much though that I'd see the girl there, in the classroom. I wanted to see her again, to find out what her story was. But they probably had all the girls sewing or cooking in an establishment such as this. My schoolhouse in Ardamet was an all-boys school after all, and that was how it was almost everywhere in the Ottoman Empire.

I could hear the muffled voice of a teacher as I was led up the creaky wooden stairs by the nursemaid. The hall was long in either direction at the top of the stairs, but the nursemaid took me left, and soon we were at the only classroom on the premises. When she opened the door I was surprised to find that my assumptions were wrong, the rows of desks were populated by both boys and girls. Maybe it was just easier to keep everyone together. And like the nurse who'd been cutting hair said before, the girls all wore headscarves, covering their baldness. The boys' heads were mostly as bare as my own, though a few wore hats. In all there must have been at least twenty children in the room, of differing ages. In all no one in the room looked younger than six years old, and the oldest looked to be adolescents.

"And here's our other new student," said the teacher, another nursemaid who spoke Armenian with a strange accent; everyone working at the orphanage seemed to have the same accent too, "Tell us your name and something about yourself, and you can sit next to Fimi."

I swallowed and my eyes scanned the room, the other children looking at me with expecting gazes.

"My name's Vartan Manukyan," I began, "I am twelve years old but I'm going to be thirteen soon, and my father is in the army. When he comes back after the war I will leave and go live with him again."

There were snickers among many in the room.

"You mean when the doctors find a way to cure death?" asked one child in the room, inciting more laughter.

"Now Hratch, be kind to Vartan, he's been through a lot, as we all have," said the teacher.

Hratch sneered; a husky boy around my age, with a large nose and thick eyebrows. I could already tell his type. He was a bully. Already he had raised my ire. My father was alive, and no one was going to tell me otherwise.

"You may call me Frau Sporri," the teacher said to me, "I'm the wife of this orphanage's director, who you may refer to as Herr Sporri. Now please, have a seat. We were just discussing arithmetic."

Frau and Herr? I'd never heard such names. Judging by her pale skin tone I deduced she was from Europe, and if so, probably from one Ottoman Turkey's allies, like Germany. But, I nodded to Frau Sporri and took a seat, glancing to my side at the girl I'd seen earlier, who'd been introduced a few minutes before I arrived. So, her name was Fimi. It was a cute name. She was staring off into space, her eyes red from crying. The teacher was giving the class a lesson on long multiplication, something I already knew.

"You are new here too, yes?" I asked her in a whisper.

She turned and regarded me with little interest, "You came just after me, now you are the newest one here."

"I suppose you're right. Did they laugh at you too when you were introduced?"

"I tried not to give them anything to laugh at," she explained.

"Are you feeling better about your haircut?" I ventured to ask.

She frowned and in a low whisper replied, "Don't you dare tell anyone I was crying."

"Everyone is bald here too you know, it's alright."

"I don't want to talk about it," she snapped.

The teacher slapped her ruler on her desk, "Pay attention!"

The two of us immediately stood up straight and faced forward. Not wishing to be on Frau Sporri's bad side on the first day, I refrained from speaking to Fimi again until the lesson was over.

Fimi

Fimi was a girl of sass and cunning. Though often separated from us by gender segregation at the orphanage, she gravitated toward the boys whenever she could. Yet that was not to say she wasn't as feminine as any other girl, evidenced by her devastation after having her hair cut. She was my first real friend after arriving at the orphanage. I was never very social, only kept a small circle of friends. But she was one of the closest. I wondered what had happened to her to put her in a place like this. I'd get some answers later that first day when we had lunch.

Once Frau Sporri's lesson concluded, we were lined up single file and taken down stairs to the dining hall, a large room with long tables and benches. A gray light filtered through the dirty windows. The seating was all very organized; we were to sit when signaled by the lead nursemaid, an elderly woman in an apron and bonnet with a booming voice. One table at a time was allowed to line up at the front of the room for lunch; whatever was in the large black caldron and some bread to go with. Though the orphanage was not run by Armenians, many of the nursemaids were Armenian themselves. We weren't to begin eating until everyone had their plate of rice from the caldron with bread and a cup of water, and the nursemaid led us in a prayer to give thanks for the meager bounty. Only after this were we permitted to eat; a few of the children snuck a bite I noticed, but they had to do so averting the gaze of the nursemaids.

To my surprise, Fimi had taken it upon herself to squeeze onto the bench beside me, though still remaining distant and not making eye contact with me. Perhaps she did have some interest in getting to know me, I hoped. If nothing else, I could tell we both were in need of a friend.

"I wonder if the food is always going to be like this," I quipped, while shoveling rice onto the bread with my fork and wrapping it up.

"I do too," she answered, doing the same.

"They change it sometimes," said the boy next to me, "Dinners are usually better than lunches."

"Good to know," I remarked.

"The first month or so here is the toughest, but once someone else shows up and you're not the newest kid anymore, you get picked on less," the boy explained.

"Oh? Sounds a bit like school. What's your name?"

"Levon," he answered, before carrying on with his meal.

I'd have make it a point to get to know Levon some more, though I got the feeling he knew his way around the orphanage well, but maybe he didn't want to sacrifice his status as 'one of the boys' by talking to me just yet. I turned instead back to Fimi.

"Do you know if the girls have a different sleeping area than the boys here?" I asked.

"I don't know any more than you do," she replied.

"I guess that puts us in sort of the same position then. Why don't we get to know one another and maybe you and I can be friends?"

Fimi thought it over, having a bite of her lunch.

"We do have something in common, don't we? Alright then, boy. Tell me about yourself."

I began telling her what village I was from, before getting to how my mother and sister had died, and finally how my father was sent off to fight in the war, and I hadn't heard from him since, but was hoping he was still alive.

"You don't think it's foolish do you? To think that my father is going to come back here and get me?"

"No, it's not foolish" Fimi answered, "My father was imprisoned. Maybe when he gets out he'll come and get me too."

She proceeded to tell me more about herself as we ate.

Fimi was twelve years old, and had always lived in Van, as had her ancestors before her. After her father had been incarcerated, for what I didn't yet dare ask as it seemed too impolite, her mother no longer had enough money to keep food on the table, or to take care of her. With no relatives to send her off to, she was brought here. I was stricken with the way Fimi related this story, with such numbness. She must have thought her home life was so miserable things couldn't get much worse at the orphanage.

"I'm sorry to hear of that," I said, not knowing how else to react.

How many other children here could say both their parents were alive? I'd always assumed that children who get sent to orphanages were, well...orphans; having lost both their parents, or were given up as newborns, not as kids around my age. It made me even sadder on her behalf, and I realized how lucky I had been to have parents who could care about me. But they were gone now. Unless my father survived the war. The point I had learned was that there always was someone worse off than me.

After lunch, the day wore on. I would not be making any other friends that day, besides Fimi. There were two more lessons, one on history and one on reading and writing. I had too much on my mind to pay much attention to them. Dinner was a little bigger than lunch; we had some lamb to go with our rice and bread. What stands out most in my memory is that first night at the orphanage. Boys and girls slept in separate rooms, each filled with rows of beds. A nursemaid showed me to my bed, and gave me a nightgown to change into. It felt strange changing in front of everybody but no one else minded. The bed was lumpy and hard, a steel bar in the middle could be felt through the whole mattress. I missed my bed at home. Then the lamps in the room were blown out, and the darkness took the room. I was able to let my emotions catch up with me, and realizing all I had lost, I finally began to cry. I was all alone in the world. Alone in a place for other children like me. The unwanted, the unloved. The survivors. I could feel bugs crawling on me, lice perhaps. The tickles kept me awake. I had no hair for them to live in now. It made me miss more than ever my old life with my father. I couldn't sleep that night. Not a wink.

The Hole

I can't sleep now either. I dwelt on this memory my first night in the camps too. The camps are a lot worse than orphanages of course, but some base similarities remain. Bad food or occasionally no food, everyone fending for themselves. The advantage Siberia had to the first camp I was in, Madekh Prison in Georgia, was that we actually got our own beds here. That prison was the first prison for a lot of inmates from the Caucasus region before they were transferred to another camp; political prisoners from Armenia were transferred there from a prison in Leninakan, as was I after staying there for two weeks. Most of the members of my gang had come out of there too.

In Madekh there would be perhaps sixty prisoners to each moldy, fetid cell, what was built to house ten prisoners originally, with not even enough room to extend your arm out in front of you. There was one bucket for us to relieve ourselves in, and it filled up fast, stinking up the whole cell. No matter the weather outside, inside it was like a steaming sauna, with a smell that would make a maggot gag. There were so many people in there that moisture dripping from the ceiling would never reach the floor. I'd have to sleep curled up on the ground in the fetal position every night, and hope that I don't fall victim to another cellmate's sexual cravings. Back then odinochka would have sounded like an improvement. If not for the Siberian cold filling this room through glassless barred windows, it actually wouldn't be so bad in here. A whole cell to myself. Imagine that. The cot may be hard and painful to the bones, but it's better than the stone ground. I even have my very own bucket in the corner. If my old cellmates could see me now. I don't even have to go back to work on building those new barracks today. Most people that get sent to odinochka get put in at the end of the day, even if they received their sentence during morning roll call. I get to just sit here for the rest of the day and not work. Sit here and freeze to death that is, but in situations like these it helps to think about how it could be worse.

What really takes me back to that first night at the orphanage right now is the thought that no one out there loves me or will miss me if I die. I either die tonight in solitary confinement, or I narrowly survive only to be sent to the Disciplinary camp. Where I will die. No one is going to remember my name. Or my deeds in life. The thought of it terrifies me. The words I've written in life may survive for some time, but I won't be alive to witness it. A sudden wave of anger sweeps me onto my feet, and I stomp around the room in circles, oblivious for the moment of the pain in my knees.

"Damn them. Damn them all. Damn Stalin! If he were here in this cell with me I'd rip his throat out! I'd tear him to pieces and watch him bleed! I don't want to just curl up and die here like a sick dog. All of that struggle, everything I have survived, for what?!"

I let out a primal shriek at the ceiling, until reduced to ragged coughs again, and I shiver. I can scream at the top of my lungs, but nothing's going to happen. I sit down on the cot and cough, gasping for breath. After trying to control the tickle in my throat, sitting silently for a few minutes, I can breathe again. I then sit with my knees drawn up to my chest, and tuck my hands into my armpits for warmth, muttering curses. The wooden cot hurts my ribs and hips, any bone I put weight onto. The walls are coated in frost. My steaming breath billows out of me as if I'm smoking a cigarette. Bronchitis, pneumonia, whatever I have, the cold is taking a toll on it. Without thinking I clear my throat, only to spark another coughing fit. I cough until I gag. I see spots swimming in the air before me and

I spit mucous onto the floor, wheezing through a congested chest. I'm not going to make it.

With the coughing fit leaving me faint, I turn over and lay on the cot in the same fetal position I used to sleep in at Madekh, defeated once again. The hard slabs of wood give me no comfort whatsoever. I shift my body, searching for a position which distributes my weight widely enough to be remotely comfortable. I try my belly. My chest can't expand enough. I try my back. Every bone contacting the wood hurts. I've no body fat to cushion anything. After minutes of shifting, I finally settle on a position where I am laying on my left side, my left knee is drawn up to my chest and I am resting my cheek on my left bicep with my arm curled up over my head , leaving my left thigh, chest and shoulder to take the brunt of the weight. But I must turn my straightened right leg upward so that my sore kneecap doesn't touch the wood. Bah. Staying in one position for more than a few minutes is torturous, to say nothing of the fact that I am literally freezing. My hands ache, my ears are numb, my nose is sore and runny. I shut my eyes, and try to imagine being somewhere else. Anywhere but here. Inevitably I revisit my past again. I'm back at the orphanage. Still being haunted by that little boy. My little brother. It's strange, I haven't thought about him for the longest time.

Raffi

Life was not so bad at the orphanage, after a while. At first it was hard to be all alone and have no one to tuck me in at night or comfort me when I was lonely or sick. For the first month I did not make any real friends, besides Fimi, who was still distant, but cared enough to suffer my presence. I didn't give up hope that maybe my father was still alive, that he just wasn't able to send word from the war front. But I learned not to be vocal about these hopes. The other orphans did not take kindly to it. Many of the children were younger than I was, others a few years older. Some of the mayriks, the nursemaids who took care of us, were as young as 16 or as old as twenty-five and orphans themselves, probably from this very orphanage. Each mayrik was in charge of twelve orphans. They acted as teachers too, though some teachers from actual schools would volunteer to come to the orphanage sometimes. In the morning we were taken to church, where we would be taught Armenian hymns and stories from the Bible. When we would return to the orphanage we would be put into a regular classroom.

Periodically we'd receive new orphans, thanks to war and the typhus outbreak. It was late December when a timid little mouse of a boy entered the orphanage while we were having breakfast. He was a rather shy child, dressed in a waistcoat over a long shirt and short trousers, with a felt cap on his head. A very European way of dressing; his family must have had a bit of money before whatever happened to them happened. The little boy was sobbing as the nursemaids seated him at a table near the one Fimi and I ate at, refusing to take food from them. Eventually they gave up and let him be.

"I've seen them cry on their first day before, but never that bad," Levon remarked.

"Wonder what happened to his parents," Fimi said.

"Must have been something pretty awful," said Levon.

"Or he could just miss them," said Fimi, "Maybe they're still alive for all we know, like mine, or possibly Vartan's father."

I didn't like her adding 'possibly' while speaking of my father, but I had since learned never to speak of him. By this time I'd even convinced Hratch that I had given up, though secretly I had not.

Many of the kids stared at the boy as he buried his face in his arms and sobbed. It was pointless to haze someone who was already so upset, luckily for him, so he was spared the teasing or pranks that sometimes accompanied being new at the orphanage. The boy was quiet throughout the rest of the day, through our lessons and through church service. I paid him little heed until that evening when it turned out he was to sleep in the bed beside mine at the end of the room. He was crying quietly into his pillow that night, wanting his mother, when I spoke to him first.

"Hey," I whispered, hoping to calm him down but not knowing at first what to say. I decided it might be best to ask what his name was and where he was from, which seemed a natural way to start a conversation, "What's your name, boy? Where are you from?"

The child looked over at me, wiping his eyes against the pillow and hugging it to his chest.

"My name's Raffi, Raffi Maghazadjian," he whispered, trying his best to stifle his little sniffs and gasps and pronouncing his last name very carefully, "I'm from Akantz."

"I'm Vartan Manukyan, from Ardamet," I answered, "I haven't been here long either. But I know a lot of kids cry on their first night."

"I wasn't crying," Raffi denied, his voice cracking slightly.

I smirked, "Are your eyes irritating you then?"

Raffi shook his head silently, still hugging his pillow.

"Just between you and me, I cried too on my first night."

"Really? But you're too old to cry."

"Don't tell anyone, but I did."

"I won't tell, if you don't tell on me," Raffi promised, "Did...did your mother and father die too?"

"My mother died a couple years ago. But my father got sent into the army when the war began."

"Is he alive?"

I hesitated. Raffi was just a kid though. He wasn't going to judge me. I decided to tell him.

"I want to believe he is alive. That maybe he'll come back and get me out of this place after the war."

"I know he's going to come find you," Raffi said, "You are so lucky, to have a father still alive."

"What about you?" I asked, before adding with caution, "That is, unless you don't want to talk about it."

Raffi was silent for a few moments, "I can tell you. My mother and father got very sick, and went to the hospital. And they never came back."

"What did they do with you?" I asked, baffled.

"They left me with the next door neighbors when they started to get sick. But the neighbors told me my mother and father were dead, and that they had to bring me here because they had not enough money to keep me. They told me I would find a new mother and father here that would adopt me. But…I don't want new parents. I want my old ones."

His voice became shaky and he clutched his pillow to his chest. I had seen two or three of the younger children get adopted since my stay here, but no one over five years old it seemed. I for one didn't expect to be adopted; in fact I hoped I wouldn't. I wanted my father to come back for me. But maybe Raffi had a chance. He was small and cute enough. Adults liked those ones.

"If you do get adopted, it won't be so bad," I told Raffi, "Your new parents would care about you and love you."

"I guess you're right. My old ones aren't coming back."

"Did you have any brothers or sisters?"

"No, it was only me. I always wished I had one though."

"Same with me," I said, "But I had a sister once…"

"Did she die?" Raffi asked.

I nodded.

Raffi stayed silent for a while, as if contemplating something.

"Vartan?" he finally asked, just when I began to think that perhaps he had finally dozed off.

"Yes?"

"Do you think maybe, when your father comes to get you…that he'd adopt me too?"

I was stunned by this question. I'd only just met this boy, and he wanted my father to adopt him? I wasn't even sure if my father was coming to get me at all, much less that he'd be willing to adopt another child if he did come for me. But this boy, who'd lost his parents and had so little to hope for, needed something to keep him going. I could see that. Just like the faint hope that my father would survive the war and find me kept me going. I had to give him some hope.

"I will ask him," I answered, "When he comes to get me I will ask him. "

"Then I can be your brother, and we can both finally have siblings," Raffi said, smiling through his tears, "You want a new sibling, don't you?"

I smiled back at him, "Yes, I do. We'll be brothers."

"Brothers," Raffi repeated, very much liking the sound of being a brother.

I didn't know if my father would be coming back for me. I didn't know if he'd adopt Raffi if he did come back. But in that moment, making Raffi smile again seemed the most important thing in the world, even if I wouldn't be able to keep that promise. From then on he was like my shadow, following me wherever I went. We were brothers.

The Hole

Raffi, he was a good kid. Raffi Mah-gha-zahd-jyahn. I chuckle before clearing my throat to stave off a cough, remembering how hard he had to try to say his own surname. He just had a few speech impediments, like a lot of kids do. My name was easier to say for him. He liked my name, I remember. He became especially excited when we learned about St. Vartan Mamikonian at church. Maybe he was related to me, Raffi would suggest.

A loud wind howls, blowing another jet of icy air through the window. I shudder violently, huddled in a ball on my cot, closing my eyes tight. If I could only sleep. This position starts to put too much pressure on my shoulder after a time, so I turn around. The same thing happens on my right side before long; and I can't lay my head down on my right side because that's where I was hit with the club.

Vartan Mamikonian is my namesake, obviously. Every Armenian schoolchild knows about him, none more so than those of us named after him. If it wasn't for his efforts to preserve Armenia's Christianity, we're told, there probably wouldn't be any Armenians today. Or if there were, maybe they'd be Muslims. Possibly Zoroastrian, if they'd clung to it as tenaciously as they did Christianity, but it's doubtful. They'd have all been killed or kicked off their land a lot sooner had they stayed Zoroastrian. Most likely, if the Armenians had abandoned Christianity when the Sassanid Persians wanted them to, they'd just be calling themselves Persians today. Interesting to think about. I wonder what 1915 would have been like in that case. But my point is, we Vartans have a lot to live up to. I can't quite say if I really have lived up to the name or not. I've tried.

I wipe my eyes and sniff. My eyebrows feel frosty. Being cold isn't getting any easier. Not yet.

Long before Turks or Russians ruled Armenia it was the Persians and Romans having their way with the country. They split Armenia between themselves, Persia getting the bigger half. The Persians weren't Muslims yet, they followed Zoroastrianism. Before Armenia was Christian they had their own form of Zoroastrianism too, but gave it up. The Persians had the idea that everyone in their empire should follow the same religion. So it follows that Christianity became a problem. Who was their king...Yezdegird? Yazgird? Something like that. I can't think straight right now, it's too cold. The Persians banned Christianity, causing Armenia to rebel. In 451, Armenia's general, Vartan of the powerful Mamikonian clan, raised an army to face the Persians. The battleground was to be at Avarayr, a large flat area in northern Iran. When Vartan Mamikonian's army finally made it to Avarayr, the Persian army outnumbered them three to one. The Persians had soldiers as far as the plain stretched out. And many of them rode atop elephants, sending a barrage of arrows down on Vartan's army.

"They rode on elephants?" Raffi asked, "How did they get elephants to take them where they wanted to go?"

I shrugged, holding the heavy history book across my lap, "Same way people control horses? I don't know."

"I want to ride an elephant one day."

"At least it's a more reasonable wish than dragons."

"But I want to ride a dragon too," Raffi retorted.

"Maybe when my father comes to get us we can go to a circus. Then you'll at least get to see an elephant. But probably still not ride one."

Raffi smiled, "I've never been to a circus. I want to see lions and giraffes and monkeys. I wish Van had a circus."

"It would be fun if they did."

"So finish the story."

"Alright," I looked back down at the book.

I wasn't reading it word for word of course, I was just summarizing the story so that it'd be simple enough for Raffi to understand. I was better at reading than almost anyone else in the orphanage, because my father taught me before the military took him away. Many of the other kids were only just learning how to read in our classes. Because of this, our teachers sometimes called on me to help with the lessons. And often after class was done, Raffi and I would stay behind and read together as we were doing now, until someone came to get us. We were supposed to be mopping the floors in the kitchen.

"Despite being outnumbered, Vartan was brave. He wasn't going to let the Persians tell Armenia what to do. He rallied his troops with a rousing speech, telling them that it would be noble to die in the name of God and country, that they should consider themselves lucky to die because they will go to heaven."

"But they won the battle, right?"

"Many people died, it says, especially after one Armenian general betrayed the others and joined the Persians. The Armenians lost, and Vartan Mamikonian died."

Raffi was silent for a few moments. The story didn't turn out the way he thought it would.

"It reminds me of the story of Ara the Handsome; he died too in his story."

I nodded, "Not all stories end happily. This one is history though. It really happened."

"If he died and lost the war, why is he a saint?"

"Saints are often people who died for Christianity," I explained, "And anyway, the Armenians kept on fighting for years after this battle until they made the Persians give up, and let the Armenians do what they wanted. The Armenians almost won, in a way."

"So that is why you're named Vartan."

I nodded, "That's where my name comes from."

"Are you sure he wasn't your grandpa?"

Smiling, I shook my head, "No. My parents just liked that name I guess."

"I wish I were named after someone like that," Raffi said, "Who do you suppose was the first Raffi?"

"I heard it's the name of a writer. My father spoke of him. But I haven't read any of his books."

"I want to be named after a hero. Like Hayk, Davit or Ara."

I suppose it was a lot to live up to, being named after a martyr. Not that it was an uncommon name. But the name carried with it a certain responsibility. One wouldn't want to be a disgrace to the name of Vartan.

"Let's go get the folktale book now," Raffi said, getting to his feet, "I want you to read me some more."

I closed the heavy book and lifted it up onto the book shelf, as a nursemaid peeked into the classroom.

"Hey! What are you two boys still doing in here?"

We turned around quickly, to be met with her angry glare.

"Get down to the kitchen, or I'll have to paddle you both, you little scoundrels."

"Yes *mayrik*," I answered respectfully, shelving the book.

The thought of being paddled had made Raffi instinctively cover his behind with his hands. It wouldn't have been the first time we'd been subjected to it, but luckily the nursemaid seemed to be letting us off easy this time.

St. Vartan

The kitchen was small, and staffed by nursemaids. Since our meals were usually quite meager, there wasn't usually a huge mess on the stove or the ovens. This made cleaning it a quick job most of the time. Often we would have nothing but pita bread or lavash, with only water to drink. If we were lucky, perhaps we'd get a side of rice pilaf, beans, lentil soup, or pomegranates and apples, but fruit was rare. Even rarer was meat. The morning after Raffi joined the orphanage, as we lined up in a row and prepared to walk from the orphanage to the church, there was a dead mule on the street right in front of our orphanage. No one was sure where it had come from or who it had belonged to. Most likely the old mule had just been abandoned after it no longer served a purpose to its owner. It would serve one more purpose to us, though. The nurses had it brought to the back of the orphanage, and Herr Sporri convinced a local butcher to come by to help them. That night we had meat with our bread.

Rumor spread among the girls that because mules are impotent they too would lose the ability to bear children if they ate it. Others were disgusted after having seen the animal in the street that morning.

"You're not really going to eat that, are you?" Fimi asked me as we sat together in the dining area, "Who knows what it died of."

Fimi continued to sit with me whenever we were given a choice in our seating arrangements. Our orphanage was generally segregated between boys and girls in most aspects besides the classroom, but nursemaids looked the other way when it came to meals.

I cut the meat up with our meager silverware and wrapped it in lavash bread, "It's been too long since I had meat. I'm tired of just bread and rice every day. If it's not going to make me sick I'll eat it."

Raffi nodded and mimicked me closely, cutting his meat in the same way.

"At least your new little pet likes it," Fimi remarked, "What is it with you two anyway? I saw him following you around at the church all day."

"Vartan's going to be my brother," Raffi said as he ate, "When his father comes back for him."

"Really now?" Fimi looked bemused.

"Raffi, I thought we agreed not to tell anyone about that," I said, speaking low, annoyed and hoping it wasn't overheard.

Fimi giggled, "You know Vartan, I didn't expect you to be the one to make friends with Raffi. Did you feel bad for him on his first day?"

"We got to talking because his bed was next to mine," I explained, eating the mule meat.

"And that's when we decided to be friends," Raffi finished with a smile, "Maybe you and I could be friends too?"

"I'll get to know you first before I decide," she answered.

We carried on with the meal, but at the end of dinner the nursemaids gave those of us who didn't eat the meat a strict scolding.

"Herr Sporri and the nursemaids worked really hard to prepare tonight's meal," the head nursemaid said angrily, "And half of you didn't even touch it. You're going to eat it whether you like it or not."

A girl raised her hand.

"Yes?"

"But if we eat mule meat, we won't have babies when we're older."

"Nonsense!"

Hratch stood up and shouted, "That thing was laying dead in the street this morning, it's going to make us sick!"

Other kids concurred.

"Silence!" the nursemaid shouted, "The meat is perfectly fine or else we wouldn't serve it to you. Food is scarce, you can't afford to not eat. Do you think you still live with your parents?"

There was a silence in the room.

"You live in an orphanage. You have to eat what you can in order to survive. I expect all of your plates to be clean, and nobody will leave until they are."

It was a speech that left a lot of kids emotional, even if they had eaten their meat. Raffi for one didn't need to be reminded that his parents were gone.

The orphanage may have been our main food source, but for those who were both sick of the food and exceptionally crafty, it was possible to find other avenues for sustenance. For instance, sometimes if we were lucky, we might even find someone at the church who would be willing to trade us some bread smuggled from our breakfast for fruit. The nursemaids tried to discourage us from making such bargains with strangers, but many of us did it anyway and were not caught.

Other times, as we walked past the market place, we might be able to take some food from the fruit stands while nobody was looking. We would have been paddled hard if we were caught. But the food was so enticing, so tempting. The morning after we were fed mule meat was a Saturday, and on Saturday mornings we were all taken to the St. Nshan Church in central Aigestan, shepherded there from the orphanage by our nursemaids. Raffi and I were walking in back of the line, next Fimi, who brought up the rear in the line next to us. Girls and boys walked in separate lines, just like they slept in separate rooms and usually ate meals at separate tables, making Fimi's friendship with me all the more unusual. The girls were taught to sew, embroider and cook, but they were also given the same education as the boys, even taught to read and write, which was not something they could usually get outside of the orphanages in regular schools.

When we went to church we stuck out; a group of around thirty bald children, some with head kerchiefs or hats but many without, dressed in whatever rags they'd been wearing when dropped off at the orphanage. Some of us had shoes, others didn't; donations of clothes and shoes from Germany and America came in gradually but so did new children. We instilled pity in the populace, making our food dealings in town much easier. They knew very well we'd come from the orphanage. A merchant might even look the other way if he saw one of us take something small like an apple.

As the three of us walked in the back of our lines, we began to talk about how hungry we were. Each of us had only bread and rice for breakfast. That was likely going to be lunch and dinner too. On our way to church the line always passed through a marketplace, with people on the sides of the street selling bread, fruit, vegetables and cooked meat. It made us so very hungry whenever we walked through there. Even if one of us had money, perhaps sent by a distant relative or found (possibly stolen from) somewhere, we were not allowed to stray from the line and buy food, or else we might get separated and lost. Today we could stand it no longer.

"I've had it," Fimi sighed, before whispering to us, "I'm getting thinner by the day. Listen; why don't we sneak some food from these merchants?"

"I don't know…" I looked around with caution, hoping a nursemaid wouldn't overhear us, "I don't want to get caught."

"See that barrel of apples coming up?" Fimi pointed to a fruit stand a little ways up the street, "I've snatched apples from there before. The shopkeeper doesn't even care. You could get one for each of us."

"But stealing is a sin," Raffi said with worry, "What if we anger God?"

"He would forgive us," Fimi reasoned, "We're orphans and we're hungry, what else can we do? I'll hide them in the pockets on my dress."

"As long as we are not doing anyone harm, I think its okay," said I.

"But what if we get caught?" Raffi asked, "They'll cane us and make us do work."

I personally was more afraid of being caught by the nursemaids, or someone else, than the wrath of God. But I wanted to set a good example for Raffi, as protective of him as I was, so I told him as long as no one was being directly harmed, it was okay in some cases to steal.

"I hope that you do not get caught Vartan," Raffi said. "But... I would love so much for an apple. Only steal if no one is to be harmed then, right?"

"Right, Raffi-*jan*. And only steal when you feel you really need to."

So, as we walked by the barrel, I quickly stepped out of line, took three apples, and quickly returned to my spot. No one had noticed; the shopkeeper had been tending to another customer. One by one I handed each apple to Fimi, who hid them in the front pocket of her dress while we walked.

"I'll give these to you while we're at church," Fimi whispered, "We'll sneak outside while they're doing their prayers and hide, eat our apples, and rejoin them as they leave."

Raffi and I nodded. This would be a treat. I felt like a delinquent at that point, skipping church to partake in sin, but I was hungry. I wanted that apple.

The church was tall, and built of stone. The interior was once decorated with paintings but these had all but disappeared. And the smell of incense strongly permeated the air. Churches are crowded places. Some might have seats up front for the elderly or handicapped, but other than that usually you'd be standing in a crowd. So once we got to the church, we stood in the back, listening to the Armenian church service and singing along with the hymns as normal. When it came time to pray and everyone closed their eyes and bowed their heads, we took our opportunity and quickly slid out the front door, and hid behind a nearby bush.

Fimi took the apples out, and we had our feast, giggling and talking amongst ourselves. We were in high spirits, until suddenly Fimi stopped smiling. Her eyes widened and she wore a look of fear. Raffi and I turned to see what she was looking at. Our nursemaid, Siran, was standing on the other side of the bush, looking down at us angrily with that stern expression only her face could make, having noticed we were gone. We were in trouble.

"What are you doing, you little devils? Come out of there and explain yourselves!"

We stood up and came out nervously, not breathing a word.

"Where did you get those apples? There are no apple trees here! Did you steal those from the marketplace?"

When all three of us fell silent, looking down at our feet, she knew we'd stolen them from the market.

"I knew it," Siran scolded, "Herr Sporri will hear of this! I will march the three of you into his office as soon as we return to the orphanage, and he'll give you each a paddling with his cane, I will see to that."

Fimi let out a helpless gasp, and Raffi looked as if he were about to cry. Being sent to Herr Sporri's office was a punishment reserved only for those who really misbehaved. I had seen very little of him since joining the orphanage, and never face-to-face and alone. He would show himself if he had something to say to us as a whole, and he'd often come to church with us. He was not a cruel man. In fact he was often very kind to us and understanding of our needs; but he believed in discipline, and consequently, corporal punishment, in the form of a wooden cane.

After she said she would take the three of us to Herr Sporri, I stepped forward.

"It was I who stole the apples, *mayrik."* I said firmly, though in reality, I was swallowing my fear, "I was only sharing with them. It was my idea, and I was responsible. Do not punish them, punish me."

I did not want to see Fimi and Raffi suffer for what I ultimately had let happen. Maybe I wanted to protect Raffi, and maybe I wanted Fimi to like me, but I did feel some genuine guilt for not refusing to take the apples. Siran was stunned by this self-sacrifice, but she believed my story nonetheless, and immediately put me to work sweeping the steps of the church as she marched Fimi and Raffi back inside. Before going into the church Raffi made eye contact with me, a look of guilt mixed with thankfulness. I simply nodded, as if to say that everything was okay, and I would now reap what I'd sewn. Raffi was innocent in all this. I was doing Fimi a big favor though, because the entire scheme had been her idea. But I thought I ought to have been more responsible, and prevented the theft from becoming anything more than just a childish fantasy.

Herr Sporri sat behind a desk in a dusty old office on the first floor of the orphanage, across from the stairs. He was a towering man, at least to me. He dressed in a long, black coat and wore circular spectacles over his eyes, his hair steel gray. His office was nothing elaborate of course. It was not as if he were profiting while the rest of the orphanage was in poverty. The office only looked slightly nicer than anything else in the building. There were pictures of his family on the walls, his wife and daughters, some of whom were also nursemaids at the orphanage, and shelves filled with books from his native Germany, many from the Red Cross, written in German, which I did not understand. And leaning against his desk was the cane; made of a lightweight wood for easy striking.

"What have we here, Siran?" Herr Sporri asked, speaking Armenian with a harsh Germanic accent.

"We caught this one stealing apples from the marketplace and sneaking out of church to share his plunder with his friends," said Siran, "His name is Vartan Manukyan, sir."

I looked at Siran and then at Herr Sporri. I was feeling nervous. I was never the type of boy who got into trouble often. When I did it left me with an unsettling feeling at the pit of my stomach. My heart felt as if it would burst.

"I think I remember this one. From Astakan, yes? So you were hungry for apples."

"Yes Herr Sporri. I stole from the market, and I know that it was wrong. I take all of the blame. My friends Raffi and Fimi were innocent. I only wanted to share with them. They were hungry too, and I care for them, so I took the apples so that I may feed them, and myself."

"Really, young man, didn't the three of you have breakfast this morning?" Herr Sporri asked, "Why would you feel the need to steal when we give you food here?"

I had not expected this question; I'd expected to simply be yelled at and hit on the bottom with the cane.

"Breakfast was only bread and some rice. We were still hungry. And we wanted to eat something different. So, I took an apple for me and two for my friends."

I could not complain about the food to his face. What would he do to me?

Herr Sporri stood up from his chair, leaning over the desk at me.

"So you would like more food and more variety in your diet," he summarized knowingly, "Fair enough. I can understand that. But does this give you the right to steal?"

"No sir. No, it does not, and I was wrong," I said, feeling the fear in my chest rising, "I will not do it again and I will be taking my punishment now. Just please, do not hurt my friends."

Siran took my arm and pulled me over to the side of Herr Sporri's desk to be caned. Herr Sporri looked down at me, and I at him. It was as if he were searching my face for honesty.

After this he looked back at Siran.

"No Siran, I've seen enough. This boy only did what he did for his friends because of our unfortunate food shortage, and he's learned from his mistake."

I was shocked, as was she. Was he really letting me go? Herr Sporri turned his gaze back to me again.

"You won't be doing that again, now will you, Vartan?" he asked.

"No, sir," I replied.

He patted my shoulder gently, "That will be all then. But Vartan, do keep in mind that our food shortage isn't our fault. We do our best to keep you children fed and healthy, but we can't do all that we would like to do. Tell your friends that too."

I nodded, a smile coming over my face. "Yes Herr Sporri, and thank you."

Siran shook her head and led me out of his office. When I made it to the classroom Raffi gave me a look as if I had just come back from being tortured. I smiled and took my seat comfortably. Of course we could not speak during our studies, but as soon as I got the chance to he could not believe his ears when I told him how lucky I'd been, nor could Fimi.

"So he didn't even punish you?" Fimi asked in disbelief, "You sure?"

"He let me off with a warning," I explained, "I get the feeling if I were caught doing the same thing again my punishment would be twice as bad as it would have been this time."

"Do you think he knew you were taking all the blame for us?" Fimi asked.

"He may have, actually," I answered, considering this possibility for the first time.

"I'm really sorry you took all the blame," Fimi said with sincerity, "It should have been me."

"I didn't want you or Raffi to get paddled."

Raffi hugged my arm. After enduring it for a few seconds I shook him off as politely as I could.

That night at dinner, after we were given our bread and lentil soup and had sat down together to eat, a familiar figure stepped into the dining room. It was Herr Sporri, and with him he carried a basket full of apples from the market in each hand. The faces of everyone lit up in excitement, but he first walked over to Raffi, Fimi and I.

"I take it these are your two friends, Mr. Manukyan?" Herr Sporri asked.

"Yes sir, this is Raffi and Fimi," I answered. Raffi and Fimi could only stare at the basket of shining plump apples.

"Well then…" Herr Sporri put his baskets down, "I guessed as long as you felt so compelled to take apples from the marketplace to satiate your hunger, I might as well do the honest thing and pay for them. Of course, since you three already had yours, these are for everyone else."

"You mean…we don't get any?" Raffi asked sadly.

"Stealing is wrong, under any circumstance," Sporri said, "I know you had your reasons, which is why your punishments aren't any harsher than they are. But owning up to your mistake was bold and heroic behavior, Vartan. You're going to be a fine young man indeed. But of course, as you promised; no more stealing. And that goes for Raffi and Fimi too."

I nodded in response, "Yes sir. "

Herr Sporri handed each child in the dining hall an apple.

"I guess at least we had ours earlier," said Raffi.

"True," I said, having only the usual dinner to enjoy now.

"He knew it was my idea," Fimi concluded, "I saw how he looked at me."

"There's no real proof though."

"Lucky for me," Fimi said with a small chuckle, "Who knows, it could have been all Raffi's doing for all they know. No one would suspect him."

"I'm glad they think it was me," I said, "I just have to stick to the rules for a while now."

Life went on in much the same way in the orphanage, for at least a few more months. In all, life at the orphanage wasn't too bad. Even if it was hard at times, I enjoyed my studies and my friendships. There was a deep unity within the orphanage. We were all Armenians, and we had all lost our parents. This unity would give us the family we didn't have. In much the same way, when we grew up we orphans would always treat other Armenians as family. We were a generation without parents, but wherever on Earth we ended up, we always had each other.

Neville Ussher

One day in February 1915, as I recall, all of the boys in the orphanage were lined up, about fifteen of us, and led down the wood plank sidewalks along the streets of Van. The girls, it was explained, were going to be taught embroidery and knitting. We on the other hand were being taken to the American Mission Hospital for something "special". The girls weren't too pleased about it, but were promised to be led in their own activities with the nursemaids while we were away.

Whenever any of us got really sick we'd be taken to the American hospital to be treated. I never got anything worse than a cold while in the Van orphanage but there had been some cases of typhus fever and the flu. The Americans were Protestant Christians and had come to preach their ways to the Armenians, Kurds and Turks. It just so happened Herr Sporri was a Protestant too, and these two institutions had an understanding with one another. Both were here for the good of the people after all, funded by humanitarian groups from foreign countries. Despite this however, the church we were taken to every Sunday by Herr Sporri, St. Nshan's Church, was Armenian Apostolic. It was likely that we were only taken to this church due to the language barrier, and besides that Sporri wasn't a missionary as was Ussher.

Raffi was full of questions as usual, with the two of us bringing up the rear of the line, under the watchful eye of a mayrik this time.

"What's at the hospital for us to go to?" Raffi asked me.

"I don't know," was all I could answer, "Keep walking."

"I don't want to get sick at the hospital," he said with worry, "Maybe I am a little bit afraid of hospitals because that's the last place where I saw my mother and father."

"Raffi, you'll need to get over that fear sometime," I said, hoping to talk some sense into him and to help him cope with his fears, "What will you do if you get very sick one day? You'll need to go to a hospital. You can't go your whole life avoiding them."

Raffi fell silent. I hoped my comment wasn't too insensitive.

"I don't want to get typhus one day like my parents," he said after we'd walked another block.

"That's what keeping your hair short and bathing is for," I replied.

"Could we get typhus in the hospital?"

"I have a feeling this trip isn't about going to see the patients," I said, though not knowing if maybe we were being put to work there because the hospital needed volunteers. I hoped not.

The American hospital was a large, white, three-story building surrounded by a metal gate, marked from afar by the American flag on a tall poll at the front lawn. America was neutral in the war thus far, hence the toleration of their presence on Ottoman territory by the authorities in charge.

We were welcomed by foreign nurses who opened the gates and led our group to the front door of the hospital, where stood a young American boy, slightly older than myself, with a woman who was his interpreter. He had light hair and pale skin, dressed in a nice khaki suit. He was stark contrast from the rest of us, dressed in our orphan clothes. He spoke with pride, first saying 'parev', 'hello' in Armenian, and telling us his name, Neville Ussher, before continuing on in his American English tongue, of which some of us thought we could pick out a word or two, though we could have been wrong. The woman, a nurse who introduced herself as Emily Turner, translated for us.

"Neville wants to greet you all, can you greet him back? "

"Hello Neh-veel," most of us said.

Neville laughed, telling us it was pronounced Neh-vull. Ms. Turner, who evidently spoke Armenian fairly proficiently, wrote on her clip board with a pencil and showed us the piece of paper.

"Here's how you should say it."

There his name was written in Armenian characters; Նեվըլ, the letters noo, yetch, vev, ut, and lyoon. Now we understood. Neh-vull. The name sounded strange to our ears, but no doubt he thought the same of ours.

"Why don't we all introduce ourselves?" Ms. Turner suggested.

Each of us gave our names and ages as we went around the room. Neville seemed to want to make an honest effort to learn our names before proceeding with our lessons. He repeated our names after we stating them, saying "parev" to each of us individually.

"Let me continue. Neville has spoken with his father Dr. Clarence Ussher and the director of your orphanage, and they've agreed to allow him to include any interested volunteers from

Sporri's orphanage in a Boy Scout troop here in Van. The troop was started nine months ago. The Raynolds orphanage already participates in its activities."

The term "boy scout" had escaped our understanding. We gave blank looks, not knowing whether this volunteer work was good or bad.

"What do we do to be scouts?" asked Hratch.

"Will we get extra food?" Raffi asked.

The nurse repeated Raffi's question to Neville in English, and they both chuckled.

"We may have snacks if the Mission can afford to spare them, yes," said Ms. Turner.

Neville spoke again, and she translated.

"In America, where he is from, there is an organization called the Boy Scouts. They formed only a few years ago. It is like a club, where you are taught skills for survival."

This idea did sound interesting, and unlike anything we had been doing in the orphanage so far. We all gladly agreed.

"Neville meets with the other orphanage twice a week and he'd like to do the same with you."

It wasn't as if we had anything else besides lessons and chores to do, so we agreed to whatever schedule suited them best. We were then led into a spare room with tables and chairs, where it was explained we would be holding our meetings. Neville seemed excited to meet us and talk about his culture back in America. I suppose being stuck in a strange foreign country made him want to create something familiar like in this instance a Boy Scout troop. No such thing existed in the Ottoman Empire.

We then found that the Boy Scout meeting was a bit like a class, but a much more hands-on learning experience. Working from a handbook printed in English, Neville first showed us several different ways to tie a knot. Some of us had never tied a knot before; some of us didn't even have shoes with laces. I had never known there were so many different ways, having only learned the basic shoe-tying knot as a child. Learning practical survival skills like this was a welcome break from arithmetic, that was for certain. At the next session Neville showed us how to build a fire using the "bow drill" method, and then we learned how to properly bandage a wound and make a splint for a broken bone. These bi-weekly excursions provided us with a welcome distraction from our own misfortunes that had led us to be placed in the orphanage, and taught us a great deal about basic survival.

Perhaps more importantly, word got around Van fast about Neville Ussher's project with the orphans in the city. Among those who would take note of the Boy Scouts were leaders of the Armenian community in Van, The Military Defense Authority, who by this time were laying the blueprints for what to do in case the Ottoman army should lay siege to the city. If it were to happen, the Armenians would be in dire straits without enough guns or enough men to wield them. They would need stores of food, water, and volunteers to do the jobs adult men would do if not busy defending the city. A troop of boys with basic survival skills would be quite the asset indeed in such a calamity. But of course, we humble orphans weren't told about the storm brewing just outside the walls of our fair Aigestan. We knew only what we were told.

The Hole

I begin to rock back and forth upon the cot, sitting cross-legged, a comforting motion that I've carried with me since my childhood days, shutting my eyes and thinking of a song for me to rock to the tempo of, settling on an aggressive, quick-paced kochari melody. I picture myself back in my apartment in Yerevan, where in my spare time I would listen to phonographs, sitting in a rocking chair as stories and poems were born in my mind. My pen and paper rest on an old wooden desk lit by a lamp, the sun filtering in from between the curtains warmly, swaying from the light breeze. A hot summer's day. Perhaps Vardavar, the holiday where youngsters splash unsuspecting strangers with water, but it's so hot that no one minds much. Answering a knock at the door could mean being greeted by a group of children with a big bucket of water. I can barely remember how it feels to be hot, to actually welcome coldness.

The need to urinate draws me out of my trance. My chest quivers and my teeth chatter, the cold piercing the windows to my cell and attacking me openly with a wrath that only a December night in Siberia can come close to. Snapping back to reality, I trace my eyebrows with my fingertips again and feel frost on them, melting to my touch. My nose is so cold I feel as if it'll fall off my face. I don't think I can feel my toes anymore. The wooden cot hurts to sit on after a long time. I await either my release from the Hole, or death, neither of which is coming soon enough. I don't know how long I've been in here now. I've lost all sense of time. But I haven't seen the sun come up yet. I've received nothing for dinner. I know they're supposed to feed prisoners in solitary confinement, but they could just as easily have not-so-unintentionally 'forgotten' about me.

I gaze over at the bucket in the opposite corner of the room, and get to my feet. It's been hours, I don't know how many, since I stood up. My knees are still sore from hitting the ground when I was thrown in. I may have bruised the bones in my kneecaps. It's what made me reluctant to get up even to relieve myself. But, while going in my pants might provide me with momentary warmth, it would freeze fast. I have to use the bucket. I limp forward toward the bucket. Dreading exposing myself to the harsh cold, I lower my pants, and hastily urinate into the bucket. It's steaming. Ah, to be so warm as to steam. It will go cold soon enough. I could try to warm myself with it, but again, it would be worse in the long run, when it freezes. Once finished, I am quick to pull my pants up again. The cold is absolutely agonizing. Is there no source of warmth in this ice cave?

That's when I look up. The lone light bulb in the room flickers dimly. Warmth. It makes me think of a star. There is a source of warmth in this room. Why have I not thought of this before? Shivering and coughing, I hobble to my cot and I drag it across the ground, directly beneath the light bulb, and I climb on top to touch the light with my hands, desperate for warmth. I remember the summer's sun in Yerevan. I used to hate how hot it got in that city. I remember getting sunburns sometimes. I hated summer. That sounds inconceivable now.

My hands are thawed by this weak little bulb, the only light in my dark world. I close my eyes and bring my face up to it.

"Hey! What is that noise in there?" a cheka guard demands from outside.

He slides open the window on the door, and sees me. He calls me names in Russian under his breath, and leaves. Seconds later, the light switches it off, leaving me lost in the darkness, consumed by the punishing cold. I clasp the bulb for any remaining warmth, but little by little, the warmth fades.

"Akh, Tamar…" I whisper to myself, slowly sitting down on the ground and hugging my sides, my hopes crushed. I feel like crying.

My mind drifts back to Van, remembering that little island they took us to once when I was at the orphanage and the old folktale that accompanied it. That's what this all reminds me of. But those days seem like part of a fantasy, something that had happened to someone else, a long time ago.

Akhtamar

It was the second Thursday in February; the day when Armenians celebrated St. Vartan's 'moral victory' over the Persians. The nursemaids awoke us before dawn, coming to each of our beds and shaking us, the early bedtime from the night before not quite compensating for being awoken at four in the morning. Blinking and then lifting my sparse bed sheets I looked across to Raffi, still curled into a ball on his bed with his covers wrapped around him like a cocoon, rebelling against all the commotion as the room filled with the chatter of around twenty other sleepy but excited orphan boys. I smirked, wondering whether to leave this problem to the nursemaids or try to get him up myself, eventually deciding on the latter.

"Hey, Raffi," I approached his bed, shaking the straw-filled mattress, "Come on."

Raffi groaned.

"Okay, you can dream about going to Akhtamar while the rest of us actually go."

Upon hearing this Raffi began to stir and stretch. He gave a smile.

"I had nearly forgotten," he said, taking his sheet off as nursemaids brought our clothes.

"You must have slept well to forget a thing like that," I remarked, "Come, get dressed."

We dressed out of our nightgowns and into our normal clothes. Raffi wore the same waistcoat and hat he'd come into the orphanage with around two months ago, but due to his rough play his pants had been patched and stitched in places.

After breakfast they lined us up in rows, divided as always by gender, and marched us from the orphanage through the streets of Van just as the sky was showing signs of dawn. The sight of thin, bald-headed orphans being led through town in lines was not an unusual sight to the other citizens. But this time, we were leaving Van altogether, traveling to the cathedral on the island of Akhtamar as an excursion so we could attend mass for St. Vartan's Day. Herr Sporri and Dr. Ussher had arranged for us to attend a mass at the famed Surp Khach cathedral, feeling it would be a good learning experience, and also hoping the sight of the orphans might be a good way to solicit donations from others attending the mass. They led the way as our nursemaids followed alongside to make sure none of us wandered off.

It felt strange to be leaving the enclosed walls of the city for the first time since I'd arrived in the orphanage the past December. Since then my world had stopped beyond those stony walls. It was too dangerous to travel beyond them alone. The talk from the adults of hordes of marauders pillaging and looting remote Armenian villages had managed to trickle down to us despite how they attempted to shield us from reality. And our orphanage was joined with increasing frequency by newly orphaned, shell-shocked children who could attest to the stories when willing to speak of them, but were usually warned not to by the adults.

"I've never been on a boat," Raffi commented, walking in front of me in the line, "Vartan, what should we do if it sinks?"

"It won't sink," I assured him.

"But I can't swim," Raffi said with worry.

"Once we get to the island you'll be so excited you won't have time to be scared," I said, though not entirely sure it would be true. Both he and I got bored at church. But at least it got him to be quiet for a moment. The boy may have had my sympathies but he could be grating at times.

We walked single file down the unpaved road leading out of the walled-in Armenian Quarter, headed for the nearby port. We could see white, triangular sails moving across the azure blue surface of Lake Van, a lake with such a deep blueness that it was almost blinding to the eyes. The rains of the past winter had turned the surrounding land green, all the way into the snowy, jagged mountains that ringed this inland sea. The land immediately around the city was mostly flat, empty plains with some gentle sloping hills; the exception being the rocky outcropping which loomed over the city, topped with an ancient fortress built by the Urartians over two thousand years ago. Living so close to such an ancient monument never failed to capture my imagination, and I wondered what life had been like in the days of kings. Like so much of ancient Armenian history it seemed like some intangible fantasy that had taken place on some other world, rather than right on the ground we lived on. But the proof of its reality cast its shadow over Van every day, as if to remind us Armenians of a day when we weren't the lowly subjects of a conquering empire. But to outwardly reminisce of such times was discouraged, even deemed unpatriotic, now that the Ottoman Empire had involved itself in the Great War.

The sun still hadn't climbed over the mountains by the time we reached the port, around an hour's walk from the orphanage. The air here was salty, you could taste it on your lips. As we walked along the docks, Sporri and Ussher stopped in front of a wooden sailboat. Sporri was dressed in the black garb of a priest, with a matching wide-brimmed hat on his head. Dr. Ussher was nearly his photo-negative, dressed all in white, sporting glasses that made him look very intellectual. Even those who needed glasses in Van rarely were able to get them, so they were an unusual sight. Both men were Protestant, but held no qualms over allowing us to visit an Apostolic church, at least in this case. The boat was manned by monks from the monastery; men with long beards and black robes.

"You will be boarding the boat one at a time," said Herr Sporri, standing on the gangplank as we lined up to board, "I will remind you again to be on your best behavior. Stay in your seats. If you start to feel seasick, tell a nursemaid and they will assist you."

Our gender-based lines merged and we were directed up the gangplank one by one. Feeling slightly disoriented by the up and down bobbing motion I glanced over the edge of the gangplank at the murky waters below. It was a strange feeling, walking above the water. I had never gone sailing before. The boat itself was just big enough for all of us to fit, though we had to sit crammed like sardines on its seats. As usual, Raffi held my hand and pushed through others to ensure we would get a seat together. It was three to a seat. Feeling generous, I allowed Raffi to have a seat on the edge so he could look over the side of the boat. To my left, Fimi managed to snag a seat. We'd been seeing more and more of her since the incident where we were caught stealing apples. I think my taking the blame for the whole thing had endeared me to her.

"How are you two doing? " Fimi asked us with a friendly smile.

She wore a dress covered in patches she had sewn herself, and a head scarf to help hide her baldness.

"I'm fine. It's refreshing to go someplace new for once," I replied.

"At least you go out more often than I do. There's still no Girl Scout troop. It's not fair." she complained.

I shrugged, "They're letting you go now."

"Because it's to church. I want to go hiking and exploring."

"But we haven't done anything like that yet," I replied with a chuckle.

All we had really done so far was go to the American mission twice a week and learn to tie knots and start fires, practical survival skills like that. This was the first real outing we'd had since the troop was formed.

"All girls get to do is cook and sew," Fimi sighed.

I didn't think it was fair either, but there wasn't anything I could say to her about it. Raffi was transfixed on the blue sea as the boat tilted up and down with the waves. The monk crew untied the boat and unfolded the sails.

"You don't feel seasick, do you?" I asked.

"No, I'm okay," Raffi said, "Just thinking."

"What about?"

"Do you remember the story about Princess Tamar and how Akhtamar got its name?" he asked.

It was a story we'd read together out of a book of old Armenian folk tales and legends. The library of the orphanage had a copy which we read whenever we had the time. I was more literate than Raffi was, so it was usually just me reading to him aloud. But I knew this story even before I was put into the orphanage. My father would tell it to me sometimes. There were a few different versions of course, but I liked my father's version.

"What's that story about?" Fimi asked.

"Want me to tell it?" I asked.

"Fimi doesn't know it yet, so okay," Raffi said, "But it's very sad, I ought to warn you."

Fimi looked at me with an attentive stare as I began to tell it as best as I could from off the top of my head.

"Once, upon the island we now call Akhtamar, there lived a princess in a palace. Her name was Tamar. She was kept there by her father, who was very determined to shield her from the outside world. Tamar used to stroll along the coast and gaze longingly across the waters of Lake Van at the mainland, wondering what it would be like to mingle with the commoners. One evening as she was on one of her walks, she came upon a boy, a commoner who swam to the island out of curiosity. Instantly she was fascinated by him, and she wanted to know everything about his way of life. And she being a princess, he was equally fascinated by her. They talked and talked all night long, getting to know one another. But Tamar was afraid of her father finding the boy and executing him. So they agreed to meet only under the cover of night. Tamar would light a torch and stand on the edge of the island, so that the boy could see her light from the shore and swim towards it. They did this for several nights, and gradually, they began to fall in love.

However, one early dawn as the boy departed into the water, the King spied them from his window. That night, when Tamar was holding her torch to lead the boy to shore, he had his guards seize her and extinguish her torch. The boy no longer had a light to guide him, and in the darkness of night he flailed helplessly, lost in the water, and drowned. People say that sometimes, at night, you can still hear his cries of "Akh, Tamar!" And this is how Akhtamar Island got its name."

After a short silence, Fimi remarked, "That was a sad story. What a cruel father Tamar had."

"Is there still a palace on the island? Are we going to get to go see it?"

"I don't think there is any palace, if ever there was one," I replied, "You know it's probably just a story."

"But if it's just a story, then why else is the island called Akhtamar?" Raffi asked, as if that logic proved the story was real.

"Maybe you have a point," I said with a smile.

"What if we hear the boy's voice?" Raffi asked, looking over the edge of the boat as if expecting to see the boy's ghost flailing in the water.

"We're not going to. Besides you wouldn't hear it during the day anyway, and we aren't going to be here that long."

"You two are morbid," Fimi said, "Why don't you talk about a story with a happy ending for once?"

I thought for a few moments, but wasn't able to recall a happy one off the top of my head "I'll look for one when I read the book again."

Though I was sure there were some, most Armenian folktales weren't especially uplifting. Perhaps centuries of being dominated had left Armenia too jaded to come up with any truly happy stories.

After a while we could begin to see the island up ahead, a green mound rising out of the sea. Not a moment too soon either, as by now two of the children had already become seasick, and had to be held over the edge of the deck by a nursemaid. The rest of us either laughed or were disgusted by the spectacle. The monks steered the ship toward a small pier on the island, and after a wait the gangplank was lowered and we were escorted from the ship in an orderly fashion. Making our way past the wooden docks, the monks led us on an uphill path, the gravel crunching beneath our feet as we passed through grassy slopes and between trees pink with early spring blossoms.

The pyramidal dome of the Surp Khach Cathedral rose to our view as we came closer. The stone structure, made of a reddish stone, almost looked like the palace from the story of Princess Tamar if not for the cross atop its highest point. Its color was a sharp contrast from the clear, mirrored blue surface of the lake and the marble white mountain peaks beyond. The cathedral somehow looked bigger from afar though, as we came closer we could see it was really only about as high as a three story building, but its proportions still made it seem enormous. It stood near monastic buildings which housed the clergy. We mostly remained silent, besides a few quiet utterances of awe breathed by some of the orphans, including Raffi. Many others were gathered in front of the church for the St. Vartan church service.

"I bet that was the palace," said Raffi, "They just turned it into a church later on."

As the monks took us around the outside if the structure they explained to us the history of the church, how it had been commissioned by King Gagik Artsruni, the king of Vaspurakan, an Armenian kingdom from almost a thousand years ago. But I only caught bits and pieces of what they were saying as I focused on the frescos and bas-reliefs etched into the red stone along the outside, each façade depicting familiar tales from the Old and New Testaments; Jonah and the Whale, and David and Goliath, and others. Raffi would tug on my sleeve and ask me what each picture meant as we walked by. I didn't always know.

The church was crowded with people who'd also come by boat on a pilgrimage to this famous church. Maybe the people in charge of the boats made sure the church never got too overcrowded by only bringing a certain amount of people over. It seemed to me an odd place to have a church, on an island. But it made it seem all the more special, somehow. Soon enough, after the monks were done talking we were allowed inside.

People removed their hats upon entering the church, and made the sign of the cross on their chests and foreheads, saying a silent prayer. We were all expected to repeat this gesture; most of us had been trained since early childhood to do this with no effort, almost on impulse, but a few others who had not been taken to church as much had to look around and attempt to copy their peers. The inside of the church seemed just as massive as the outside. All over the walls and ceiling were frescos, chipped with age, depicting more stories of the Bible. The creation of Adam, the temptation of Adam and Eve, and their downfall, the life of Jesus, his apostles. It all seemed so very ancient. Like we had traveled back several centuries to when the church was new. Because the church was so old, the paintings were worn in places, but in others it was remarkably visible. The altar was adorned with incense and decorations, a picture of the Virgin Mary holding baby Jesus before a large decorative cross. The dome on the ceiling stretched up forever. This was to be a most interesting mass indeed.

Raffi, Fimi and I couldn't stop looking up at the pictures as we stood near the back, by large trays of water and sand in which people placed candles. The pews were near the front of the church but there weren't many, and were reserved for people that have trouble standing up. I've always been transfixed by candles, so I watched as they melted into one another, some lurching forward and dousing themselves in water as if to put the fire out on purpose, others placed so close together that their flames became one, and the melting wax sealed them together. I would root for the smaller ones to keep burning until eventually the water put them out. I also listened to the sermon while entertaining myself; it was about Vartan Mamikonian's struggle to preserve Christianity in Armenia. A story I already knew well, so did Raffi. But of course what stands out most in my mind these fifteen years later are those frescos, those paintings. I'm not up on the times, I don't know if that church has been reduced to rubble or turned into a mosque yet. It'd be an awful shame. But why not destroy it, everything else is gone now.

After the service we sang a hymn, and it was adjourned. I'd be telling Raffi stories all the way back to Van after this, I was sure. Biblical ones. Ones where the hero got a happy ending. Ones far-flung from the way things seemed to work in real life, at least in our short, unhappy lives. Once the liturgy was finished we filed back onto our boat, leaving this mystical island behind.

"Did you want to tell me another story?" Raffi asked.

"I'd like that too," said Fimi, "But, maybe one without ghosts this time."

"Alright Fimi," I chuckled, "Any suggestions Raffi?"

"How did Armenia first become Christian again?"

This was a tale we'd been taught at the orphanage, and had heard about in church. I think Raffi just wanted to hear my retelling of it. It was a story mixed in myth and historical fact, though it had been presented to us as complete historical fact. No one questioned it, not even the adults.

"I'll give you the version that's easier for me to remember," said I.

The story began with a history of the Armenian royal family's feud with one of the noble nakharar families. Lots of violence, assassinations and bloodshed. It was hard to keep all of it straight.

"First the dad of St. Gregory the Illuminator, Anak, killed the king. The king was Khosrov the Second I think. As punishment the new king had St. Gregory's whole family killed, but Gregory escaped and lived with a distant relative somewhere else. Prince Trdat III was just a little boy, and he went to Rome to go to school, and be taught the pagan ways. Gregory grew up raised by Christians, and became a Christian. Years passed, and St. Gregory decided to go back to

Armenia to preach his religion. He later came to be King Trdat's assistant, the king not knowing that Gregory's father killed his father."

"How did the king not know?" Raffi asked.

"Gregory must have been secretive about it. "

"It helps that everyone thought Gregory's family was completely killed off," Fimi added.

"Yes it did. He also kept his Christianity a secret for a while too. Things went well until Gregory refused to make an offering to the goddess Anahit. King Trdat was insulted, and after Gregory told the king who he was and that he was a Christian, Trdat had him tortured and thrown into a deep dark pit for thirteen years."

"The book had all the gross ways he was tortured in it," Raffi told Fimi with a chuckle.

"Let's skip that part, please," Fimi requested.

"This one part has them pour a bunch of water down his-"

"She doesn't want to hear it, Raffi," I interrupted.

"I remember it from church anyway," said Fimi.

"Aw alright, " Raffi said, "Well tell me, how did St. Gregory live for so long in that pit?"

"The king's sister felt pity for him, and threw him a loaf of bread every day," I answered, "So for many long years Gregory waited. Sometime during the wait, a group of Christian nuns fled Rome into Armenia. Among them was the beautiful Hripsime. King Trdat III fell in love with her when she and the nuns were captured and brought to him, but she refused to marry him because she was a nun. She resisted him with all her power and some say Jesus gave her the strength to fight the king off. When the king gave up trying to make her his wife, he had her tongue cut out…"

Fimi put her hands over her ears, "I thought I made it known that I wanted you to skip these parts."

I smirked, teasing her, "Oh, I forgot. Well in any case, Hripsime got tortured to death, and the rest of the nuns had this done to them too. It was then that the king's soldiers started acting like devils and going insane, running through the forests and tearing off their clothes. And God was so mad at the king for killing the nuns, that He turned him into a wild boar."

"Is that part really true?" Raffi asked.

"I guess God can do anything," I answered, "Whatever He likes."

"But you have to be really bad like King Trdat for him to turn you into a boar, right?"

"That's right. He wouldn't do that to just anyone who sins, they have to be really bad. Next, the king's sister had a dream that St. Gregory would be able to cure the king. And so, not knowing if he would be dead or alive, she had the guards pull St. Gregory out of the pit. And miraculously he was healthy, and looked great for having been there for thirteen years. He prayed for God to forgive King Trdat, and finally God answered the prayers. He turned the king back into a human, and from then on King Trdat became a Christian, and he made Christianity the religion of all Armenians.

Everyone destroyed the pagan temples, and from then on, Armenia was Christian, and the first Christian country in the world."

The Hole

It was tempting to believe in these tales, because they represented an escape from the way things really worked in this world. The bad people got their comeuppance. The story we were told made it seem like everyone in the country voluntarily and eagerly converted to Christianity overnight. It seemed so simple. Later on I'd learn about how many pagans were forced to convert or die. Trdat III and St. Gregory led a campaign of religious persecution against their own people. That's what it was, if you really think about it. Mythology and history from the pre-Christian era was destroyed or reinvented. Holidays and folktales hijacked and given a Christian overhaul. In some isolated pockets Armenian paganism survived for centuries more, but it eventually all but vanished. The Armenian pagans must have felt the same way Christian Armenians felt under Islamic Ottoman rule...at least before the killing really started in Turkey. And maybe if some of their ancient temples and statues had been preserved Armenians wouldn't need to work so hard to prove they'd been in eastern Anatolia longer than anybody else, and certainly longer than the Turks. We might have had buildings and monuments every bit as grand as those in Greece or Egypt. But since St. Gregory had them all destroyed, we'll never know that they even existed.

I can't completely fault Christianity though. The Armenian alphabet was invented so that priests could translate the Bible into Armenian, after all. And without that alphabet I do believe the Armenian identity would have been lost. It really should have been invented sooner though. The alphabet was subsequently used to record Armenian history through a Christian lens, in an effort to make what is ultimately a foreign religion imported from Israel

"Armenian". Hayk, the legendary forefather of the Armenians, was now descended from Noah. Ara the Handsome, a king who died in battle and was originally said to have been resurrected by magical dogs, was now replaced by a look-alike after his death, because only Jesus is allowed to be resurrected. If only the original tales had been written down. So much history lost, because the only literate people around were priests.

Despite having been the first country to accept Christianity, it seems like God left the Armenians to fend for themselves a long time ago. Though Armenian history had its highs and lows after Christianity was adopted, I'd venture to say Armenia's conversion to Christianity was where the downward spiral began. Not long after that, Rome and Persia divided Armenia up, and it became a prize for every single empire to stomp through the area since, most recently the Soviet Union. When Armenia was pagan it conquered more than half the Middle East under King Tigran the Great. We were mighty, invincible. Look what turning the other cheek got us in the end. It ultimately landed me in the Gulag, in this frozen cell. All of these events, over almost two thousand years, coincided to put me where I am now. Where was God in all of this? If there is a God, He must just like to tell sad stories, stories like what happened to Princess Tamar and her lover.

It's not hard too difficult to imagine why I wonder about God, is it? Of course at this point of the tale, my imaginary audience, you haven't heard the half of what happened to me. But I was already starting to get a little bit doubtful about God by the time I was thirteen and had lost both of my parents, before the Great Calamity even hit us. And now what should I think? Here in this dark cell, no food, no water, just ice. I cannot sleep. I just lay on my back, on this hard wood cot, more a table than a cot really. My breaths ragged, my body shivering uncontrollably. What sort of kind God would put me here? Sure I've done bad things before, just like anybody. But why do I deserve this? I think I have the answer. It's not that I deserve it, but my being here makes a certain amount of sense, if you try to think like God. I will tell you all my thoughts on God from this isolated cell, in time.

I am not an atheist. Not really. I've had my doubts in the past, but in my adulthood I have come to answer my own questions about God for myself in a way that makes sense to me, and I think, though I don't know, that there is a God. Even if I did lose my parents, and everything else. Even if I am locked away in this cell to die, die for my dream of a better Armenia. God is supposed to be all-knowing, all-powerful and all-good. How then, does evil exist in the world? How did the Turks seemingly get away with what they did to the Armenians? How did any other of history's equally bloody episodes go unpunished? I've been told it has to do with letting humans have free will, but I do not find that explanation satisfying in the least. What about natural disasters then? Earthquakes, volcanoes, floods, famines, diseases? They've killed millions. Couldn't God have saved those people? There must be more to it. I think I know the real reason God lets terrible things happen to good people, and lets the evil-doers get away with it, at least until the afterlife, if there even is one.

God is a storyteller.

God is like me, a bard. He likes to tell stories. The universe is his setting, living creatures are his characters. Each of these creatures has their own story. Some happy, some tragic, some neither. God allows evil to exist because it makes his stories much more interesting. There's no point to a story if there's no antagonist, right?

Or at least something to struggle for or against. It makes perfect sense. He can still be all-knowing, all-powerful and all-good. Does telling a sad story make him bad? He's just the author. Go; tell your own sad stories. Are you to blame for what happened to those characters in your story? No. If you are a storyteller, you are simply compelled to tell whatever story that comes to your mind, be it with a happy or sad ending. Though your characters, if aware that they're characters in a story, would likely curse your name as soon as something bad happens to them. Maybe even decide that you don't exist.

But I could be completely wrong. Krikor for one would hear none of my far-fetched religious ramblings when we discussed them in our bunker at night, ever the Orthodox. He says that I am no longer Christian, that I have strayed from the righteous path, and he's not the first person to say this to me. But this is the only justification I can think of, if a single omnipotent deity exists in the universe. It is also why I tend to call myself agnostic if anybody asks. I could easily be wrong in my attempts to understand the mind of God, if there is such a being. I am but a humble speck in this universe. There is much that I can't know, that I will never know. It would be arrogant to think otherwise. But, if by chance I'm at least on the right track toward the truth, I am flattered to have made my brief cameo in God's tragic tale. He created the setting and all of these more important characters, but still remembered to include me. Humble though I am, I can't help but wonder if the storytellers, poets and musicians of the world had some of that godly creativity rub off on them in the creation process. Each character in a story has aspects of the storyteller in some way, after all. Us bards, we are the Gods in our own universes.

Tork Ankegh

"Long, long ago, there once was and was not a giant who roamed these lands. His name was Tork Ankegh. He was as tall as twenty men. He had the strength of forty men, and when he ate, he ate as much as forty men."

Raffi watched me from his bed with great interest, clutching his pillow and sitting cross-legged on the bed in his night gown, his face reflecting the lone flickering candle on the little table between our beds, as I rehearsed from memory tales we'd read from the book of Armenian folktales from the classroom in the orphanage. After months of telling stories to Raffi before bedtime, I was beginning to memorize a lot of them, and Raffi didn't mind hearing them again and again, though he delighted in hearing new ones too. These old folktales and fables were one of the ways Raffi and I had learned to cope with the loss of our parents, as we'd both grown up listening to them. We were onto our fifth one tonight, but we had to be quiet, or else a nursemaid might come in and scold us for not being asleep.

"Wow, he ate as much as forty men?" Raffi repeated in astonishment.

"That's what they say."

"How did anybody have enough food to feed him all that?" Raffi asked.

There was a snicker from Hratch, in a bed nearby, "You'd eat that much if the orphanage had that much food."

"Would not." Raffi retorted.

Hratch often liked to heckle us, though not in an outright aggressive way. He'd listen in on my stories sometimes, only to berate them for being too unrealistic and fantastic. He liked to be the one to burst Raffi's bubble, who often took any story I told him as the absolute truth.

"Anyway, let me get back to the story," I continued, "The mountains would shake if Tork Ankegh yelled, and it would frighten the animals. Flocks of birds would fill the skies when he roared, flying away in fear. And if he lifted a large boulder and squeezed it, it would turn to sand in his hands."

Raffi, trying to visualize it, put both his hands in front of him and made believe that he was squeezing a rock into sand, rubbing his hands together afterward. I had to admire having that kind of imagination.

"However, Tork Ankegh was a very friendly giant. He loved the Armenian people and their land. He would rise to their defense when they were in danger, or under threat from evil doers. One time, when an angry dragon descended from the clouds and set fire to their crops, an Armenian village asked Tork Ankegh for help. Tork Ankegh climbed up Mt. Ararat, where the dragon lived. The land quaked when the two of them fought, but Tork Ankegh wrestled the dragon to the ground with his bare hands, and broke the dragon's neck."

"He did that to a humongous dragon all on his own?" Raffi asked.

"Well you have to remember he was a giant."

"Why did the dragon set fire to the crops?"

I didn't really have an answer for him. "The book I read this story from didn't say why."

"I know it didn't. But, why do you think the dragon was so angry?" Raffi implored.

"I don't know. Maybe the people did something to make him mad."

"People are always killing dragons in these old stories. Maybe they're mad about that." Raffi guessed.

It was a good point. But you're never meant to sympathize with the dragon. The dragon burns villages, kills people and kidnaps princesses. You're not supposed to wonder why. Dragons are just another villain among the mythical creatures that inhabit Armenian folktales. A creature there only to serve as a villain. Only Raffi could come up with these kinds of questions, with his open-minded way of looking at the world.

"Maybe they were. But, that was just one of Tork Ankegh's many exploits. Another time, when enemies tried to attack Armenia from the sea, the people called on Tork Ankegh once again, and he sunk all of their ships by lifting boulders and hurling them from the sea cliffs. He freed Armenia, and as long as he lived, no enemy dared get close to Armenia."

"It's too bad he's gone, huh? We could sure use a giant to help us now," Raffi remarked.

I didn't like Raffi worrying about things like that. We learned of the Great War in school, about how our country, the Ottoman Empire, was at war with the Russians and allied with Germany. Not just my own, but many of our fathers had been drafted into the Ottoman army to fight, never to be heard from again. But increasingly over the past few months, the orphanage began receive many more new orphans, orphans from some of the same surrounding villages we were from. But they did not lose their families to conscription or the typhus outbreak. The nursemaids told them never to tell us what had happened to their families. I suppose they did not want us to worry. We were children after all; we did not deserve to fear for our lives. As a result, a lot of the newer kids never spoke to anyone else at all. These poor souls had lost their families to slaughter, and had somehow made it to the city of Van from the rural villages in the province. It was a miracle any refugees made it out alive at all.

Hrant

Hrant was one such new kid to the orphanage. The boy now slept two beds down from me. I could tell there was something different about him when he first showed up at the orphanage during mealtime. He had a blank, emotionless stare when the nursemaid introduced him to us. It didn't seem like anything could reach him. He was dressed in typical impoverished village rags, and his darkened skin betrayed a young life spent working in the sun. Certainly someone from outside the city. But, for the first couple of days, he didn't talk to anyone. Maybe because he was told not to upset the other kids, but more likely because he just couldn't bring himself to.

Sometimes, in the middle of our lessons, he'd burst out in tears and have to be escorted out the room by a nursemaid. He also had a bad habit of wetting the bed each night, and got teased pretty hard because of it. One boy received a bloody nose and a black eye in response to their teasing. Herr Sporri had to paddle Hrant for that. He was prone to random outbursts of anger and aggression. Still, normally no one really solicited much of a reaction out of him with teasing alone. He was plagued by something else. This piqued my curiosity, and I wanted to know more. I had taken to collecting everyone's story in the orphanage, but I knew somehow his would be unique. So one breakfast, I made up my mind to sit someplace different, near him. Raffi of course followed, even though I didn't really want him around for this.

"Can't you go sit by Fimi? Just this once I want to sit somewhere different."

"But I want to be by you," he whined.

"You can be apart from me for a few minutes can't you?"

"Why don't you want to sit by me?" Raffi asked, feeling offended no doubt.

"I want to see if maybe I can get Hrant over there to be our friend too."

"That kid is kind of scary. I have never seen so much blood when he beat up Shavo for making fun of him."

"I think he just needs someone to talk to."

"Okay, but can I still sit by you? I won't get in the way."

"If you stay quiet, then maybe I'll let you sit with me."

I always ended up giving in. A few moments of solitude were too much to ask for since Raffi came into my life.

Eating bread with hummus and beans off of a steel tray, I casually inquired to Hrant, "What village are you from, Hrant?"

Hrant looked up from his meal, giving me a cold glare, "I don't want to talk about it."

"Well why not?" Raffi asked, butting into our conversation, and going against his agreement, to my annoyance.

"Because I am not here to entertain little asses like you."

Raffi gasped, "You're not supposed to call people that."

Hrant shoveled beans into his mouth with a spoon, in silence.

"I apologize for Raffi," I said, "I just thought, maybe you'd like to talk about it. It might make you feel better."

"Were either of your parents murdered?"

Raffi and I were silent, before I shook my head no.

"Then it's a lot sadder than anything that's ever happened to you. You'll never know what it was like. At least until the soldiers of Jevdet Bey come here, for the rest of us."

"Who?" Raffi asked.

"Mr. Bagdasarian," said a nursemaid, surprising Hrant by walking up from behind, "I believe you've said enough."

"Yes, mayrik," he said, continuing to eat while glaring at me.

"Maybe we should go sit with Fimi," Raffi suggested.

I sighed, and picked up my tray to go sit at our usual table, leaving Hrant alone.

Orphanage

Everyone knew something terrible was coming. The calamity had already arrived at the surrounding villages. But none of us, possibly not even the adults, could have anticipated the sheer magnitude of it. Yes, it would be nice to have someone like Tork Ankegh to protect us.

I told Raffi, as we sat at bedtime telling stories, "We'll be safe here in Van. Don't you forget that, no matter what the other kids say."

"I know, that's what you always say. But even the grown-ups are scared about what might happen. You remember what we heard the cooks talking about, that one night?"

Three nights before, Raffi and I had been mopping the dining area after dinner, which was one of the chores we were meant to do when we heard one of the nursemaids talking with two of the cooks about it in the kitchen.

"We need to start serving less bread. Who knows when we'll get more?" one of the cooks said.

"We'll be lucky enough to even get our share with those beggars looking for food to eat," said the elder cook. She was an old woman. She lamented, "All of those sad refugees coming into town from the villages with their tales of horror. Who knows when they'll come for us here in Van?"

"You don't think they could come here, do you? I mean a city as big as ours? They couldn't possibly…I'm sure things will turn out alright," said the nursemaid, as if to convince herself things would be alright.

"Well you remember what happened twenty years ago. If Jevdet Bey says he's going to get rid of us, then he's going to try," said the elder cook.

"I still don't see why our army would turn on its own people," the nursemaid said with a sad sigh.

"Jevdet Bey is a psychopath, just like the other Turks in charge. We're not 'his people'…we're Armenians," answered the elder cook.

My mopping had slowed to a standstill as I listened to their conversation. Raffi looked up at me with a curious look on his face.

"What is it Vartan? What happened twenty years ago?" Raffi whispered.

"Nothing, Raffi, it's nothing. Let's finish mopping these floors," I replied.

I knew, of course, what had happened twenty years before. I had heard enough stories from my family. It was a mass killing of thousands of Armenians in the empire, when Abdul Hamid II, the Bloody Sultan, was in power. But Van had held out, surviving being put under siege. That didn't mean there weren't still tens of thousands of deaths in Van anyway. A lot of the nursemaids were orphans of that catastrophe, which was something still fresh in the minds of many of us in Van. Only the very young, like Raffi, were blissfully unaware of it. Everyone thought things would get better, that it would never be as bad as that again.

"Why are they talking about giving us less bread to eat?" Raffi asked with concern. "And who's Jevdet Bey? Is he the one who killed the families of all the new kids?"

Questions. Raffi was always so full of questions. This time, they were questions I did not want to have to answer for him.

"I think that they are scared that bread will become harder to get very soon. They want to save the bread so they have some for later," I explained, to the best of my ability, "And Jevdet Bey is the governor of the Van Villayet, the region where we live. Raffi-*jan*, I do not want you worrying about these things anymore. They're for adults to worry about, not us. And if there is a bread shortage and you're really hungry, maybe I will give you some of my bread."

"Oh…thank you, Vartan," Raffi said, hesitantly continuing to mop the floor. "I know I will not go hungry with you around, but save some for yourself too."

"I will be sure to remember to, don't worry."

Since that night I could tell Raffi had been growing wearier. So had I. By trying to calm Raffi down I was at the same time hoping my own words were true. It was part of why it was nice to have a surrogate little brother around. I almost got to regain some of the innocence I had lost by that time, though only five years his senior.

"Don't worry about what the cook said. Adults just worry a lot." I said dismissively.

"But I can't help it," Raffi protested.

"Our city is surrounded by walls, no one will hurt us," I assured him, "Besides, this is a big city. We don't get bandits or marauders here like there are out in the countryside. So let us just get some sleep now. I am tired."

Raffi groaned, "Aw, can you tell me just one more story? I wanted more stories. I want to hear the one about Zangi and Zarangi again."

"There will be time enough for that tomorrow, Raffi," I promised, blowing the candle out, on the little table between our beds.

Raffi put his head against his pillow.

"When is your father going to come back to get you, and adopt me?" Raffi asked, in a low sleepy voice.

"I don't know. Whenever he can, I guess."

Raffi asked this question from time to time, usually as we were going to sleep. The truth was, I wasn't even sure if it was going to happen, and if it did, I didn't know if my father would even take us both. He was barely able to care for just me before he was drafted. But at this point, I wasn't going anywhere without Raffi. It would have to be both of us or neither of us. My father would have to understand, once he returned to get me after this war business was over with. My father was coming back. My father was alive. Every day my hope for his return grew smaller and smaller, but I had to keep it alive in my heart.

As I lay hoping and wishing that my father would return to get me and Raffi out of this orphanage, Raffi had gone silent. As always, he was more tired than he believed himself to be fifteen minutes before. I turned and rested against my pillow, drifting into an uneasy sleep.

Tuesday, April 20, 1915

I slept soundly that night, the night of April 19th, the night I recited the story of Tork Ankegh. There are certain moments in my life that I remember so vividly it might as well have happened yesterday. I can't remember every day I spent at the orphanage, for instance, mostly I remember specific episodes, some more fully than others. And I scarcely remember dates, especially ones that happened fifteen years ago. But this day... I will never ever forget. This was the day when everything in my life changed. I could never be the same. A part of me died, and I was reborn. Reborn as an adult too soon. Far too soon.

The sun had barely risen over the mountains when the city of Van erupted with the sounds of gunfire and cannon blasts. My eyes shot open, awakening with a shock. Everyone in the room was jarred awake by the calamity outside. Many of us screamed, cried or tried to hide ourselves under the covers. Raffi jumped into my bed and clung to me for safety. Neither of us said anything as he held onto me, both of us cringing when the sounds of cannon blasts erupted. We could feel the very walls shake. There was nothing I could say. I thought we were about to die.

The nursemaids rushed into our sleeping quarters.

"Come children! Get out of bed! Come downstairs!" they shouted, each of them pulling us out of bed, forcing some boys out from under their covers. A few had to win a tug-of-war first to get the covers off. As a nursemaid approached my bed, I pulled my covers down, not wanting a battle, just wanting to leave the room for someplace safer. Raffi held on tighter, looking at me as if I were crazy for wanting to leave the bed.

"Raffi," I whispered, "Come on, let's go."

"No," he whimpered.

"Come, quickly," the nursemaid urged, pulling Raffi off of me as the small boy struggled and whined, yelling at her to let go of him, fearing for his life.

I got out of bed, and as soon as I stood up Raffi ran to me, and a nearby building was rocked by a cannon shell. The nursemaids quickly herded us all downstairs, still in our nightgowns. My heart raced, and I almost believed that I was having a nightmare. This just didn't seem like it could really be happening. There were more screams as a stray bullet shattered one of the windows in the room. No one was harmed, but there was a large pile of shattered glass on the ground, and the ceiling now had a smoldering bullet hole.

We were immediately brought down to the first floor of the orphanage, and to the dining hall. The girls in the sleeping quarters across the hall from us were also evacuated, as the nursemaid herded dozens of frightened, nightgown-clad children down the stairs and into the dining hall. We were not in our usual orderly, single-file lines. It was a mad rush to get downstairs. Raffi and I were pushed and shoved; I nearly lost my footing on the stairs. Once we entered the dining hall we were instructed by the nursemaids to huddle beneath the tables, which all of us quickly did. The air was filled with the sounds of gunshots and explosions. The staff and the nurses were all busy trying to calm the children. Herr Sporri entered the room as well and could be heard giving orders to the nursemaids in German, among them his own wife and three daughters, telling them what they should do with the children.

"They're going to come for us now, aren't they?" Raffi asked me, in tears because of his fear, "Jevdet Bey is coming for us now!"

"Raffi, " I answered, holding my little brother close and speaking into his ear so he could hear me over the noise, "I don't know what's going to happen, but whatever does happen, I'm not going to leave you behind."

I couldn't think of what to tell Raffi to calm him down now. The words would not come, perhaps because I was just as terrified as he was. Eventually Fimi found us and crawled beneath the table to be with us. The room itself was too noisy to talk to one another. We could only exchange looks. We would remain in this room for hours, with no food, able to do nothing else but wait and listen to the war going on outside. We were too afraid to even use the bathroom. Many children ended up soiling themselves.

After a few hours of agonizing waiting, Herr Sporri brought in two men dressed in military uniforms and wearing fur caps. They were Armenians.

"Listen, children!" Sporri shouted, and in moments the orphans quieted down, waiting for Sporri to continue. When he did, he was calm, but firm, projecting his voice over the noise outside, "As you no doubt have realized, this is an emergency. The Turkish army has surrounded the Armenian quarter of the city. I want to assure you that because this orphanage is a German facility, we will be safe in here. As many of our newest orphans have witnessed, these are dangerous times outside of the city walls. It is my deepest regret that you children should have to bear witness to this; I myself had instructed your nurses to keep this horror from you so you would not panic, but now I am afraid it is beyond my control."

I remember feeling a tinge of anger when he told us this. How long had he known something like this was going to happen? Why hadn't he prepared us for the worst?

"The Armenian resistance is short-handed, I'm afraid," Sporri continued, "Those of you who are in Dr. Ussher's Boy Scout troops, you may be some of the few young men left in the city with any survival skills or first aid knowledge. For this reason, you will be answering to these two men. They will escort you to Dr. Clarence Ussher's hospital to rendezvous with boys from the other orphanages where you will do as they tell you. As for the girls, you may be put to work in other ways if needed, but for now you are to stay here. No one is to leave this building without an adult. No one is to go to the upper levels of the building. There is sufficient danger from gunfire and cannonballs, which are more likely to strike the upper levels. It is my understanding that work will be done to fortify this building and others in the city. Now then, this is Mr. Ara Kotanyan and Mr. Shant Avetikyan, the two men who are going to be in charge of the Boy Scouts until the fighting ceases."

The children stared and listened, none of them daring to make a sound as Sporri gave his orders. Both of these men had been injured in one way or another; Shant wore his arm in a sling, while Aram wore a thick bandage around his hand. Perhaps that was why they had been put in charge of us rather than defending the city with the others.

"Every able-bodied man in the city is fighting, " began Kotanyan, "We only have around 1,500 men defending the city from Jevdet Bey's army, and not enough guns for them all to carry. We haven't the sufficient weaponry or ammunition to hold the Turkish army back for long. Because of this our city will need any help it can get. It's a matter of survival. It has come to our attention that Dr. Clarence Ussher's 'Boy Scouts' have been taught survival skills over the past few months. This is why we need you. Some of you will be collecting ammunition which you will bring to us, some of you will be in charge of putting out fires and helping to fortify buildings, still others will be helping put the wounded onto stretchers and tending to them at the American hospital, which is severely understaffed and in need of volunteers. There is little time to train you, but you will learn what to do as it happens. Those of you who are not sick or injured will get dressed and we will take you there."

Some of us were rather timid about getting up and actually setting foot outside under this siege, but our people needed us. Raffi clung to my arm as we said our farewells to Fimi and followed the other boys. I had a feeling this was the last time I was going to see her for a long while. Certainly we'd been taught a lot in Boy Scouts, but in the mayhem that was going on around us I don't think there was a boy among us without fear in his heart and I doubted that we mere children would be able to make much of a difference in a situation like this. We had our clothing brought to us by the nursemaids and were led into the common room to change, the girls staying behind in the dining room.

Soon after we were changed our clothes, Kotanyan and Avetikyan opened the doors, with pistols drawn in their uninjured hands. It is quite possible they may have only had one bullet apiece; all of the pistols and rifles in the city, which were very few in number because Armenians had been forbidden to carry them, were in the hands of its defenders. The two men went ahead of us, making sure it was safe before they led us down the street, and we followed them in two single file lines. Herr Sporri and a nurse followed behind.

When we exited the building, we were immediately met with a gruesome sight. The bodies of four people, two men and two women, lay in a pool of their own blood right there in the street in front of the orphanage. They had bullet holes in their heads. These were the first dead bodies I had ever seen. I looked to Raffi, who stared at the bodies in stunned silence. The Great War had finally reached our doorstep. The adults must have known that it was useless to tell us to look away. These wouldn't be the last dead bodies we were going to see.

The narrow, twisting streets of the Aigestan district, normally teeming with people at this time of the day, were now empty and devoid of life. The only signs of people came from dead and bleeding bodies. Everyone else was barricaded inside their homes. Buildings were full of bullet holes, and some were heavily damaged and crumbling because of cannon blasts. Men could be seen crouching on rooftops with guns pointed over the city walls, shooting only when they could get a clear shot. The sound of guns and cannons was deafening and ceaseless. For our first trip to the mission during the siege, we could do nothing but witness the chaos. We had neither stretchers for the dead and wounded nor any means of putting out fires. We were surrounded by a nightmare. It seemed as though the city was bearing witness to the end of civilization. Our world was crumbling around us. Where was Tork Ankegh now?

The Hole

The harsh coldness billowing through the barred windows has been piercing me for hours now. I can feel the ice on my eye lashes. My fingers are numb. It's getting harder to move them. My feet feel the same way. They are cold, even through my boots. But now, it's as if I'm beginning to free myself from Siberia's icy grip. The shivering has slowed. When it stops, that's when it's supposed to set in.

Hypothermia.

I welcome it. I'll feel warm again when it sets in. If I could only get to sleep, maybe the night would pass more quickly. I may never wake up from this sleep. But I don't really mind. My story ends in Odinochka, I know that now. Krikor the priest can pray for me all he likes. It's never helped me before. I doubt that it could help me now.

The winter nights in Siberia are long. It may only be 9 o'clock, 10 perhaps. But it has been dark for a very long while. I was thrown in here after lunch, many hours ago, unless I've lost my sense of time. I don't know how many more hours of this blistering, pitch black coldness before the sun rises. Even if I survive three nights of this, it's off to the disciplinary camp for me. I don't know how it's supposed to be worse than a Gulag, but that is what I have heard about it. I am not going to make it through this. There is only one escape from this cell, only one escape from the Gulag. Death. Stalin has turned the entire country into a Gulag.

The world is a Gulag. We are all serving a death sentence; time and method of execution unknown.

It's too late to tell anyone my story now. I may not see anyone else as long as I live. I never realized I would regret it this much. After all, I never became a storyteller so I could reflect on reality, on this prison I've been trapped in since I was born. I tell folktales and fables. I write poems about the pleasures in life, color, tastes, and scents. I tell stories with fantastic creatures, heroes which vanquish evil. I tell them because they're my only means of escape from this prison. In my fantasies, heroes rise to greatness and protect the weak. In the real world, heroes are thrown into Gulag camps. Or marched into the desert to die. And villains are treated like gods.

I don't want to tell stories about stone walls, barbed wire fences, armed guards, barren tundra. Nor do I want to conjure up the horrors of my youth; a story of famine, loss, bullets and blood. But because I chose not to tell it, the story is lost. Erased from history. Fit to be denied by the very villains who caused the tale to be so miserable. When I am gone, I will be reduced to a number. A statistic among thousands. No one will stop to think that each tally mark has its own story. I understand that too late now. If I ever do get out of here, telling my story will be the very first thing I do. But, alas, my heart tells me that this is the end. I'm finally making that prison break.

Laying back on the hard cot, with my knees curled up to my chest, all I can do to pass the time now is to dwell on that past which I've kept buried all these years, back to that day in 1915, when the calamity began, when my innocence was shattered. It's something I try never to think about. But, at deaths door, I can do no more but reflect on my life. I close my eyes. I can smell the gunpowder, I can hear the bombs, the screams. It is April 20th, and the Turkish army has surrounded the Armenian quarter of Van, demanding that all adult males be surrendered. They call us rebels. If resisting our own wholesale slaughter is a rebellion, then perhaps that's what we are. For those of us who are too young to understand what was going on, well, our childhoods will come to an abrupt end. We couldn't be children anymore. We had to mature or die.

Siege

After being led from the orphanage to the American mission by Armenian resistance leaders a few hours after the bombardment began, Dr. Ussher and his son Neville awaited our arrival, and we entered the building. Because it was an American building it was neutral territory, and therefore we were told by Dr. Ussher and his translator that the Turks would not fire upon us here. For a few minutes, Herr Sporri and Dr. Ussher seemed to have a rather grave conversation in English. I could not understand what they were saying, though I could pick out certain terms, and I knew they were talking about Jevdet Bey. Troops from other orphanages in Van were arriving too, and we all gathered in the main lobby. Wounded citizens were filling the other rooms. It would likely get much worse from then on. Raffi and I had become very quiet after our walk through the city. We were both appalled and frightened. Orphans from the Raynolds orphanage and others around town were arriving as well, brought there by men who were for some reason or another unable to fight. When it seemed like all of the orphans had arrived, Dr. Ussher began to explain what we were here for and what we were to do.

"I would like to make it clear that you are here today to aid your community in this dire time," Dr. Ussher began, speaking to us in English. "Our hospital on these neutral premises is for civilians alone. We are treating neither wounded Armenian fighters nor Turkish soldiers. Your work aiding the Armenian soldiers will not be in conjunction with this Mission. But, some of you may be assigned to work and stay here in this hospital as helpers, due to the low number of men and women available to do such menial tasks. We will divide you into separate troops based upon differing tasks, and each troop will rotate between jobs from day to day. May God be with you in this trying time."

A woman beside him repeated his speech in Armenian so that we could understand. I could see why Dr. Ussher wanted to remain neutral and not bring in those directly involved in the fighting, rather than suffer the wrath of the Turkish army too, but it was still obvious that his sympathies were with the Armenians.

But we were still frightened and confused. They wanted our help in this? We were just little kids! Sure we knew how to tie some knots and such but what good were we in this situation? This was something for adults.

Raffi and I were first placed into a troop of perhaps ten other boys, most of whom I had never met before because they were from other orphanages, and our first task was to fortify buildings. Raffi and I were a little antisocial in general, and weren't even well acquainted with some of the children in our own orphanage, but our friend Levon was among our troop, and Hrant was there too. Shant Avetikyan was the one to lead our troop to our first mission, a fedayi fighter chosen because he'd injured his arm, and he couldn't join the resistance as a fighter. He wore his arm in a sling, but he was still an imposing figure. Shant had a dark complexion, prominent mustache and wore the uniform of an Armenian freedom fighter. He was a good friend of Aram Manukyan, leader of the Armenian resistance. Upon hearing of Aram Manukyan I wondered if we could be related, but alas there are many Manukyans. Perhaps we had a shared ancestor in the distant past. Someone named Manuk.

"Your community appreciates your efforts," Shant told us all as he led us into town, speaking over the constant gunfire, "We're going to St. Nshan's Church. It's near the center of Aigestan, away from the walls of the city. We will be safe there. We need to help fortify the building."

It was the same church we always went to, so we knew the way. But it felt very different from the streets we walked before. The bazaar where I had stolen apples for Raffi and Fimi was empty, desolate. It was hard to imagine how such a drastic change could happen overnight.

As we made it halfway down the dusty, abandoned streets toward the church, glass shattered from a second story building. I pulled Raffi away from the falling shards. More bullets hit the side of the building. Shant rushed us along, telling us to hurry away. He turned a corner and we followed. He stopped us, and checked us all to see if we had any cuts. No one had been hurt.

"We will continue," he said, taking the lead again, "Those bullets hit the second story of that building, but if you see any bullet casings on the ground as we walk to the church I want you to bring them to me. We're collecting them and recasting them for ammunition."

"What's a bullet casing look like?" Raffi asked.

"They're small, brass cylinders," Shant answered, "You'll know them when you see them. And another thing; pray it does not ever happen, but should a cannonball land near us and not explode, you are to douse it with water right away, to prevent it from exploding. And then bring it to us; we can make use of the gun powder inside."

This instruction made many of us uneasy. None of us had any experience with firearms, and Raffi's question only served to voice what little we knew about what was going on around us. As we traveled to the church we could spy others digging trenches in the streets and boarding up windows. How quickly our fair city had become a war zone.

Finally we reached the church. Largely empty at the moment, save for clergy and a few families and individuals who hadn't the time to make it home before the fighting started, this would serve as a place of refuge to many more people once it could be fortified. An old man with a wheelbarrow full of mortar greeted us as we arrived. His mule hauled a wagon of bricks and stones, anything he could have hastily picked up and loaded there.

"So these are our helpers then?" he asked.

Shant nodded, "Yes, the ones from the orphanage. They have a little training, but we'll see how well they handle this job. This is their first field test."

"They look like a fine group of boys," the man said, looking at us, "I'll show you what to do, and then you can take over. I have to get back to my shop and mix mortar for other buildings."

I began to find it strange how thoroughly planned out our defense against the attacking Turks already seemed to be. Maybe tensions had been simmering for longer than I realized. In the shelter of the orphanage I had only been able to gather an inkling of what was really going on, making it seem like this conflict had developed almost overnight. But as I understood it, a similar siege happened just twenty years ago, maybe the older townsfolk were simply reprising their roles from that conflict.

The old man showed us how to spread the mortar over the bricks and stones, and invited us to give it a try. Thus the long, grueling process of laying bricks around the church began. The sounds of gunfire and cannon blasts echoing across the city didn't make our job any easier either. Aigestan was not very big; a cannon from the fields outside the city walls could reach any point on the quarter it wanted. And one stray bullet could mean an unexpected death to any of us. We did have some help with our tasks. The priest and his clergy were there to help with the heavier stones, as were refugees staying at the church for shelter, mainly women and children. Between Raffi and me, I would lift the stones and place them after he spread the mortar, as did the rest of the smaller children.

We worked on fortifying the foundations of the church by building short walls of stone and mortar for the remainder of the day, taking a break at noon only to eat. Our brows dripped with sweat. We didn't say much; there was nothing to say. Only that twenty-four hours ago we had no idea we would be doing this. Shant oversaw our work, but with his wounded arm he couldn't partake in it himself. He was a stern leader, and pushed us to work faster, but he was not overly strict and if we really needed to we could rest. We were joined by other civilians who were staying there for shelter, very soon Armenians from other parts of Van were fleeing to Aigestan for safety, and the church would take in all that it could fit. But because food was scarce and nobody wanted to brave the chaos of the city, we had to rely on the food supplied at the church we were working at. And unfortunately the only things they had to eat at the church were communion bread and wine.

"We will be getting more food delivered after nightfall," explained the priest, Father Der Harutyunyan as he handed us each some bread, "The baker didn't want to risk making the trip during daylight, and we were quite unprepared when the fighting broke out this morning, I am sure you can all understand."

"Why is this happening, Father?" asked Levon, who'd been toiling along with us this whole time.

It was a question on all of our minds. The priest looked struck by the question, not knowing exactly how to answer.

"God is testing our spirit and our faith, dear boy," Father Der Harutyunyan answered finally, assuming Levon was asking a spiritual question.

"I mean why are we under attack?" Levon pressed, though trying his best to remain respectful, "No one has bothered to tell us. We only awoke to all of this going on."

"Ah, I didn't know how much had been told you in your orphanages or by Dr. Ussher," he said, a nervous chuckle, "You see the Ottoman army wanted some four thousand able-bodied men from Van to join their army. But when they asked this question in nearby Armenian villages in recent days…every one of the conscripted men were later killed. There have been other such massacres across the country. Armenians were banned from carrying guns; so when the army attacked them they had no way of defending
"

There was an uneasy silence.

"We don't want to let the same thing happen here," the priest concluded, "And so, we are defending ourselves. Now of course, I don't believe you yourself, nor any other child, will be called on to do any fighting, we just need all of your help to take care of those not fighting."

It seemed Father Der Harutyunyan had done a better job explaining what we were doing here than anyone else had up to this point. But he still wasn't telling us the full scope, that this was the beginning of an extermination campaign; we'd find that out for ourselves later. After we received our bread, the priest brought us small cups of wine; just enough to wash it down. There was a little water to go around of course; we had a bucket of it on call in case of any fires or cannonballs, but I think that the adults wanted to treat us as if we were adults too, and thus as a symbol of our newfound maturity, we were offered wine. Besides that, we had to make do with what we had. We couldn't drink all the water and have none in case of an emergency.

"I've never tasted wine before," Raffi said as the priest filled a small cup with wine and gave it to him.

"It is holy wine," I said, "They do give it to children during communion. But if you have much more than that small amount, you're going to get drunk."

"I wonder what that's like." Raffi asked.

Just as he did, one boy in our troop named Armen took a drink, and immediately spat it out.

"Mine's gone bad!" he exclaimed.

Raffi sniffed his cup and took a drink. Immediately his face scrunched up and he gagged, but swallowed it.

"It's burning my throat! It tastes disgusting!"

"It's supposed to taste like that," Shant explained.

I eyed my glass, and decided to take it all in one gulp. I coughed and wheezed, it burned in my throat just as it did Raffi. I can credit that experience for my never trying alcohol again until I was in my twenties.

"How do grown-ups drink it?" Raffi asked.

Shant just chuckled, "We'll get more water from the well, we'll just need someone to volunteer to bring it to the church."

The priest then led us in a prayer, and we then ate the flesh and blood of Christ for lunch. I suppose he wouldn't have minded, given the circumstances.

Once we finished eating, it was straight back to work. We continued to work in silence, listening only to the sounds of warfare in the background. Raffi was laying mortar as I went to pick up a large stone on the ground.

"What's wrong with being Armenian?" Raffi asked me, "Why don't they like us?"

I could scarcely answer that question any better than Raffi could have.

"We don't follow their religion," I answered, "We have a different language too. "

"So it's because we're different?" Raffi asked.

"I can't think of another reason, and it doesn't make any sense to me either, Raffi," I answered, lifting a heavy rock onto the wall. I winced, feeling a pain in my lower back.

"Lift with the knees, not the back," I heard Shant say to me. He would say this again and again to us, as most of us had never been tasked with lifting heavy objects. This was advice I would take with me in the Gulag; I still hear his voice telling me that at odd times when I'm working and lifting things.

The Church of St. Nshan

As the day wore on in an agonizingly slow pace, more and more people from outside Aigestan, parts of Van which were not so well protected, showed up at the church seeking shelter. Those who were able joined us in building fortifications around the building. Buildings across Aigestan were getting similar treatment, usually by those who lived there. Local brick layers supplied the mortar, and worked throughout the day. Everyone whose job wasn't to feed or nurse gave up their jobs and helped with the resistance, and if possible, like the brick layers, used their trade to our advantage. Tinsmiths, coppersmiths, blacksmiths, jewelers, anyone capable of doing so were making bullets with which to defend the city. The entire town joined the effort. We believed that if we could just outlast the siege, we would be liberated by the invading Russians from the east. Luckily we had the higher ground; Castle Rock was within our borders, and many of those who had guns and could shoot them were stationed there.

But, these were all bits of information I learned from hearsay during or after the siege. Though we knew more about why the Turkish army was bombarding the city than we did when we woke up to it, we still didn't know much by the time evening fell. I was beginning to dread the idea of walking back to the orphanage in the dark, when Shant gave us a welcome reprieve.

"You have all done great work, young men" he said, "It grows dark now. The food supply should be here soon, so I think we should go inside now. We'll stay here until morning, and then we'll rendezvous with the other troops at the American Mission and switch tasks."

We welcomed this. Our hands and muscles were sore, and some rest and food were just what we needed. The wall would help protect the building from bullets and explosions. It was a safety zone we had created, and we were proud.

The inside of the church loomed large. It wasn't quite as decorative as Surp Khatch, but it was still impressive. A painting of St. Nshan dominated the ceiling. There were two rows of pews at the front, occupied by families that had set up camp there. The rest of the church was open; the candle trays had been moved against the walls to make more room. When the food arrived, prepared by bakers and farmers who'd worked around the clock since the siege began, our troop was called upon to disburse it. We were given baskets of bread, milk and eggs, and told only to give one serving to each person. Though hungry, no one asked for more than their fair share; but perhaps this was because the siege had only started that morning. No one was starving yet. After dispersing all of the food, finally we were allowed to eat.

Our chores that day left little room for small talk or anything of that nature. I could tell by watching Raffi though that he was both fearful and confused by the chaos going on around him. He was just going through the motions like the rest of us, though only eight years old.

Shant approached the two of us as we ate, holding two brooms.

"When the two of you are finished, I'd like you two to sweep up the dirt in the church," he said, pointing to the doorway where a lot of dirt had been tracked in from outside due to our building the fortifications outside, "The priest would be most appreciative. Sweep from the doorway down to the altar."

"Yes sir," I replied, and Raffi nodded.

I didn't know why he'd elected us. Maybe it was because out of all of us Raffi and I were always together, and they needed two sweepers. Such a burden it was sometimes, having a little boy follow my every move when I was already exhausted. But, we were experienced sweepers thanks to the orphanage, where every individual could be expected to be put to work sweeping or mopping the floors at least once a week. So, we did as we were told. Raffi and I began to sweep the floor of the church, as refugees and other scouts set up their sleeping places on the floor or on the pews.

"We're going to lose all of the good spots to sleep because of this," I grumbled.

"Are we going to have to sleep on the floor?" Raffi asked.

"Probably, the families got to the pews first," I sighed, "All the more reason to make the floor clean I suppose."

"I've never been to church at late night before," Raffi said as we dusted the doorway, and made our way down the main aisle.

"Yes, but you've slept at a church before, haven't you?" I remarked.

We both shared a laugh. Laughter was a more powerful weapon than guns or cannons in this situation.

At least, until one of those actually hit.

At that very moment we heard a crash through the ceiling. In the instant between that and the impact into the floor, I grabbed Raffi and we both fell forward on our knees. The people inside the church screamed and gasped. A large cannonball had fallen through the dome of the church and crashed into the floor, making a crater exactly where Raffi and I had been standing only moments before. If it had exploded we might all have died, but it did not. I slowly got up and helped Raffi to his feet as he shuddered. Another boy ran towards it with a bucket of water and doused it before it could explode. Steam rose from it. Shant and the Priest rushed over, and after the cannonball simmered, for a few moments, they took it out from the ground using gloves, the Priest having to do the brunt of the work because Shant had one hand to use.

"Calm down everyone," ordered Shant, "Was anyone hurt?"

Luckily, it seemed that no one had been injured. But people were still screaming or crying out of shock. The loudest screams were coming from Hrant, who was huddled in the corner, in complete hysterics.

"They're coming for us, it's happening again, not again not again!!" Hrant screamed, crying and continuing to rave.

An adult, someone from the clergy, tried to calm him down.

"Get away from me!" Hrant yelled, shoving the man away and hiding in the corner.

"Leave him,' said Shant, "He will calm down on his own."

Shant turned to Father Der Harutyunyan, "I'll take it to where its gun powder can be extracted. But I may be in need of some help to carry it."

"I am certain someone here will assist you, I will ask around," said Father Der Harutyunyan.

"I'll leave you in charge of the boys while I'm away, Father," Shant said, "Keep close watch of the boy in the corner. "

The two of them carried the cannonball outside.

"I guess we're done sweeping the floor…" Raffi stammered.

"Are you alright?" Levon asked from the pew he was sitting at, in awe over the entire thing.

"Yes, we are," I replied.

"I skinned my knee when Vartan pulled me down," Raffi said, rubbing his kneecap.

Hrant was still sobbing, the loudest noise in the church.

"Is he okay?" Raffi asked.

"It's just Hrant, he's always been strange," said Levon.

"No, he's been through something like this before," I said, looking at Hrant, "Something worse."

The three of us stared at Hrant, who was facing the wall bawling, imagining what the Turkish gendarmes must have done to his village.

Levon turned to us, changing the subject, "You two are lucky, that cannonball could have landed on you."

"It almost did," said Raffi.

"We're all lucky it didn't blow up," I said, "Or this church would be rubble."

Raffi hugged my waist tightly when I said that, as if he finally realized what could have happened had the cannonball not been a dud.

"There's still a little space on the pew next to me for you two if you can squeeze in," Levon offered.

"Really? Thanks, I wasn't looking forward to sitting on the ground."

There wasn't enough space for us to both lie down, since we were sitting next to a family of three, two parents and a small child, but we could sit down and try to curl up off to the side with our knees bent, and barely fit on the pew. Over time Hrant calmed down, but stayed in the corner, staring blankly at the stone wall.

"What if another cannonball hits the church?" Raffi asked as the two of us tried to get some sleep.

It was time for me to try to ease his mind, even though I had those exact same fears.

"It could have hit anywhere in town. There was such a small chance of it hitting the church; I doubt it will happen again. It would be like lightening striking the same spot twice."

"Can you tell me any stories?" Raffi asked, laying down in my lap and curling up.

It struck me that our last story was Tork Ankegh, the night before. Was that really only twenty-four hours prior? It may as well have been a million years ago. Another life ago.

"Perhaps I can tell you what I remember about Davit of Sasun," I offered.

"I've been waiting to hear that story," Raffi said with a small yawn.

"The story is told as a poem, I remember back home a bard would rehearse the whole thing every winter to the others in the village. All I remember is the story of it though; I can't remember it word for word."

"Tell it to me anyway," Raffi requested.

I began as best as I could at the time, though I could not truly do the epic poem justice. The tale begins with the King of Sasun, Lion-Mher, regretting in his old age that he has no heir to take the throne when he dies, due to his queen being unable to conceive. There are other stories dealing with Lion-Mher's youth and adventurous exploits, but I did not know them too well yet at the age of thirteen. Everyone knew about Davit of Sasun though. I summarized the story for Raffi's eager ears, doing my best to inject some life into my basic retelling for him like the bards would have done.

"As the story goes, Lion-Mher was visited by an angel who told him that his queen will bear a son, but in exchange for bringing this new life into the world, both of them will have to die. The king agrees, and nine months later Davit was born, and his parents died. With Lion-Mher dead, and no one to take the throne, Sasun was invaded by the forces of Egypt. Sasun's new king, and Lion-Mher's brother, Big-Voiced Ohan, surrendered to the Egyptians, and Sasun's citizens were forced to pay them a lot of tribute, like cattle and wheat, things they needed for themselves."

"That's mean," Raffi murmured, "What about Davit?"

"Davit himself was sent to live with his uncle Big-Voiced Ohan. Growing up, Davit was told nothing of his past due to the wishes of Ohan's wife. She was weary of Davit, because she thought Davit might try to take the throne from Ohan when he got old enough."

"Well he should have been the king," said Raffi, yawning again and getting comfortable. I had wanted to curl up too while sleeping, but it didn't seem like Raffi was going to let me do that. I silently begrudged my own commitment to making this ordeal easier for him at the expense of my own comfort.

"I know he should have been king, but Ohan's wife liked having her husband in power. She was mean to Davit. He was sent outside most of his childhood, befriending wild animals. One day he thought he could bring the animals home with him. The town was in a panic because he brought back wolves and bears, all kinds of scary creatures he befriended."

I expected a response to this humorous episode in the epic from Raffi, but he was fast dozing off.

"Alright Raffi, I'll continue it tomorrow. This is the kind of story you need to pay attention to."

"Mmhmm…what's going to happen next?"

"Well, next he meets an old hag in the woods, who tells him about his father. Once he learns about this Davit decides to become a warrior, take back his throne and fight the Egyptians so Sasun can be free."

Raffi gave a light smile, with his eyes closed, "That's what you're going to do one day, Vartan. You're going to be a warrior, and free us all."

I gave a half smile, and patted my little brother's head.

"St. Vartan helped you today, when the cannonball fell down. He knows you're going to be the new St. Vartan."

Such an imaginative child he was, Raffi Maghazadjian. Even after all he had been through today, even the Turkish siege and a narrow brush with death would not remove the innocent smile from his face. Perhaps he was right and St. Vartan was with me, who am I to say? After the horrific things I have seen and experienced, I do not understand higher powers, angels or God. I try to, but I do not. The bitter years between 1915 and 1930 have done much to rid my mind of such simple, childlike acceptance of God. I question why he runs the universe the way he does. But what little remains of my inner child would like to believe maybe something was looking out for me that day in the church.

The next day we rose early, Shant needing to shake some of us awake so that we could get moving at the earliest possible opportunity. Waking up was painful that morning, to be taken from my blissful dreams and thrust into a chaotic, frightening reality. I gently patted Raffi's head, and he squirmed and groaned.

"We're leaving, Raffi."

"I don't want to leave the church today," he murmured, "What if a bomb falls on us?"

"We'll be alright, Shant will be with us."

Raffi sighed and sat up from my lap. We got up off of the pew. Shant lined us up, making sure we were all there, before moving us out. Another troop would cover the church soon enough.

As we exited the church, and made our way to the Mission to rendezvous with the other Boy Scout troops, I looked back at the damage done to the church by the cannonball. It had knocked the cross off the top of the dome. The cross now sat on its side in the dirt, splintered. Never to dominate the skyline of Van again. Thus, the Turks did their best to chip away at our several thousand year presence in the city. Perhaps there would come a day when there were no more crosses over our fair city.

The Hole

As I got older, I was able to better contextualize what was happening in Van during those times. I've met many former citizens of Van in Armenia, who came over as refugees after the war. They knew much more about what had been going on in April of 1915 than I, thanks to being either older when it happened or living outside of the orphanages. It was true that Jevdet Bey had tried to force the Armenians of Van to provide them with conscripts for the war, and the Armenian community refused because they had heard what Jevdet did to other Armenian villages where this demand was made. Wholesale slaughter. The weekend before, six villages near Van had been razed to the ground and its citizens exterminated. Those who had survived these massacres came to Van for refuge, and told their tales of horror there. After the massacres orchestrated by the Sultan Abdul Hamid beginning in 1894 during which Van had also been under siege, the massacre of thousands of Armenians in the city of Adana in 1909, and the sporadic pogroms that had taken place in the Van region since February, it wasn't hard to believe Jevdet had his eyes set on the city of Van proper next. Twenty thousand Armenians died during the 1896 siege of Van. They weren't about to let that repeat itself.

As it turns out, the reason we were awoken by gunfire so early in the morning was that the battle had actually begun right in front of our orphanage. Turkish soldiers had begun fill trenches around the Armenian quarter the day before. Around six in the morning on April 20th, two Armenian women were seized by Turkish soldiers in the street outside the orphanage. When two Armenian men, perhaps their husbands or brothers, tried to intervene, they were shot and killed. Theirs must have been the dead bodies that greeted us as soon as we stepped out of the door on our way to the Mission. Hearing the gunshots, the Turkish army outside the walls took this as a signal to open fire. And somehow the Armenians held them off with what little they had; some old rifles and pistols, very little ammunition, and a lot of improvisation.

All of this against the backdrop of the Great War, amid fears that the Armenians within Turkey's borders would join Russia in destroying the Ottoman Empire. The Turks had been looking for an excuse to rid their country of Armenians for a long time, and here was the perfect one. These "evil" Armenians in Van were rebelling, in hopes of backup from the Russians! Surely the rest of the Armenians in the country were going to follow suit. An entire race of people was labeled traitors. An edict was issued by Jevdet Bey. All Armenians were to be exterminated, and any Muslim caught harboring Armenians in their home would witness the Armenians being put to death, followed by their own family and themselves. I've heard stories of a few Muslim Turkish or Kurdish families risking it; from my prison mate Avedik for example, whose family was rescued by Kurds in the city of Kars to the northeast of Van, around the time this was happening. But unless it was out of the genuine good in their hearts, there was little incentive for local Muslims to protect their Armenian, Greek or Assyrian Christian neighbors.

The adults were more prepared and informed than us unfortunate orphan children. They knew a storm was on the horizon long before the rumors slowly trickled down to us. I can't say I blame Sporri for keeping some secrets from us of course, but surely he must have come to regret sheltering us so once we were taken from the orphanage to be used as volunteer units around the city. Even during the siege, within the city's walls we were still sheltered to some degree from what was really going on outside them. We didn't have to see very much death at first. Once refugees started coming into the city though, we'd get a taste of that. It would have ultimately benefited us to know what we were up against and why. Then again, I still struggle to understand the why part. I don't think I understand it any more than Raffi did back when it was happening. I suppose you could blame the Great Calamity on the evil sides of organized religion and nationalism. Or perhaps on human nature. Yes, the biggest tragedy of all when I think about it is the fact that both victim and perpetrator were human. Humans divided by petty, intangible, self-constructed differences. A species that would do such a thing to itself shouldn't be allowed to walk this beautiful Earth and defile it.

But God just lets it be, looking the other way. And whenever I ask a religious man why these things took place, they tell me God was testing our faith. A test of faith? Is that what this is, God? Is that what my life has been all this time? These frost covered walls, this dark cell, this prison where more and more people die each day, all a part of your game? Am I your 20th century Job? Well, you've lost your wager with Satan in my case. Some storyteller you are!

I break into a coughing fit, finding that I've shouted these last few sentences aloud. I hope the guard doesn't come back.

Perhaps God's wager worked better with other Armenians, who despite going through hellish hardships remain strong in their faith, even under Stalin's watchful eye. Perhaps they prefer not to think too hard about why God lets evil deeds befall his followers when he is supposed to be all-powerful, and just go along with whatever their preacher tells them because anything else is heresy; perhaps they remain true to their faith out of loyalty to their heritage or their ancestors who also endured centuries of enemies trying to convert them; or maybe they remain Christian just to defy both the Turks and the Soviets, who would have them be Muslim or atheist, respectively. None of these are valid reasons to follow a religion. To keep faithful to a religion only because it isn't what your enemies want you to do is the same as letting them decide your faith for you. If you are going to be a Christian, do so because you truly believe what is in the Bible, after reading it very thoroughly, cover-to cover, and asking yourself if it really helps you make sense of this horrible world. If it does, then good for you. You are a real Christian. To truly choose between Christianity and Islam you ought to read both the Bible and the Koran word for word and then make your decision. But no one other than secular scholars do that. I on the other hand find it hard to reach any conclusion. To be either strongly religious or strongly atheist requires an equal level of narrow-mindedness, and I find myself somewhere in the middle.

Religion is a stupid thing to kill one another over. As is nationalism, another of man's idiotic concepts taken far too seriously. What is a country? It's all just lines drawn on the ground, territorial pissings. Human beings are no better than a gaggle of tree monkeys fighting and killing one another over fruit. Actually, I must rescind that thought; fruit is tangible and needed to survive, ideas are not. Humans are therefore worse than monkeys; they kill one another for reasons that make less sense. But both species are fiercely territorial. Soviet nationalism is perhaps the worst I've seen. Here we have a country where you can be sent to death camps for thinking unhappy thoughts about Josef Stalin, our "glorious" leader. Stalin is no God. He's as human as the rest of us, only his cowardice and paranoia are far above average. His power is just an illusion. In a few decades, he'll be gone. Just like the Young Turks and Jevdet Bey. A black stain on history. Thank God, they're dead. It never lasts forever, these nationalist delusions. They'll just be replaced by something else.

Sometimes I wonder if the old gods; Anahit, Vahagn, Aramazd, the ones Armenia followed when it was a strong empire, would have taken better care of us than God has.

Levon

The subsequent few days were spent doing our duty to our city, being trained as child soldiers, except we had no guns. There weren't many guns to go around, and if they were going to give them to anyone it needed to be someone who knew how to use a gun. A few of the teenage orphans from other orphanages knew enough about how to shoot to be given an antiquated pistol, and be sent down to the trenches just on the other side of the city walls. Shant wanted to train us in how to shoot so that we could defend ourselves if the worst came to pass, but there just weren't enough guns or ammunition to do so.

Eventually, we were given wooden replica rifles to practice holding. Shant would take us to trenches behind city walls, where we would have drills, learning how to aim and how to position ourselves in case it was ever left up to us to defend the city, if worse came to absolute worst. Some of us were more enthusiastic about this training than others. Despite being clearly made of wood, we were instructed to treat them as if they were real. We learned the proper way to hold it, resting the butt of the rifle in our shoulders, closing one eye and leaning our cheeks against it as we aimed and kept it steady, even how to breathe as we pulled the trigger. Raffi liked pretending the gun was real and making gunshot sounds when he pulled the pretend trigger. If we got too playful we'd get a harsh scolding from Shant though; this was a life or death situation. There was one such incident between Levon and Raffi as I recall, just as we were leaving the trench to our next assignment.

"Hey Raffi, put your hands in the air!" Levon exclaimed, aiming his wooden rifle at Raffi.

"Never!" Raffi shouted with a laugh, and he pretended to shoot Levon.

Levon clutched his chest, "You got me."

He then staggered, and fell to the ground, in humorous convulsions. Shant marched over to the scene, clearly furious. He picked Levon up roughly by the arm.

"This is not a game!" he shouted, slapping Levon across the face, "Jevdet Bey's army is going to kill us all if we do not defend ourselves! If we lose our men, it will be up to you! How long do you think you can last if you keep treating your gun as a toy?"

Raffi hid behind me, and we quickly tried to join and blend in with the rest of the boys, watching as Levon got a verbal lashing that almost reduced him to tears. We never played with our guns after that.

Our chores rotated from day to day, but I made sure Raffi never left my sight no matter what it was we were doing. This wasn't too hard to do of course; the boy was almost constantly holding onto me or following so close behind me that whenever we were suddenly told to stop walking he'd slam into my back when I stopped. The only other two boys in our troop that we knew were Levon and Hrant, who we might get a word out of occasionally when we weren't busy working, Levon more often than Hrant. Levon didn't socialize as much after getting in trouble with Shant though. Meanwhile, Hrant's mental condition hadn't really improved any since his breakdown at the church, beside the fact that he was again silent and numb rather than hysterical.

Levon was a good kid, and had a good head on his shoulders. We weren't as close as I was with Raffi, but he was always there to shine a rational light on our situation. He had been in the orphanage a great deal longer than most of us, but he was still humble. His parents had given him up for adoption when he was too young to remember, so the orphanage was all he knew. Perhaps that was better than remembering who your parents were and how you lost them, a pain most of the rest of us had to deal with everyday.

We didn't return to the orphanage at all those first few days of the siege. Those of us working far from the American Mission were often forced to sleep where we were, in as safe a spot as we could find. On the third day of the siege we were busy helping someone board their shattered windows, when a cannon shell exploded a few houses away. It landed in someone's garden, taking out a fence and shattering several windows, sending debris through the air. We ducked, and were showered with pebbles and small rocks. The fire was spreading quickly.

"Get the bucket!" Shant ordered, "Bandage the wounded! We need to get some more water!"

The bucket had been placed along the sidewalk, and since Levon was closest he darted for it, straining to carry the heavy bucket toward the flaming home, even if there was little hope combating the fire with such a miniscule amount of sand in it. I'd emerged largely unscathed, though the pebbles landing on my back had hurt. A boy in our troop named Vatche was hit with a larger rock, however, and was bleeding from his head, screaming.

"Get down!" Shant shouted, pulling those closest to him to the ground and looking in Levon's direction.

It happened so quickly. The next bomb landed in the street right in front of Levon. The sound was so loud I thought my ears would bleed. More debris was hurled in the air and smoke shrouded the whole street. We didn't know what had become of Levon. We could hear gunshots coming from nearby roofs; Armenian fighters retaliating to the blasts. It was then that Shant darted into the smoke, searching for Levon. The rest of us stayed down, or found shelter.

After a time, the dust finally settled, and the weapons fell silent. Neither side of the conflict wanted to needlessly spend ammunition. One by one we got to our feet. I stood, helping Raffi up, both of us coated in a layer dust. We could see Shant not far down the street, crouching beside the crumpled form of Levon, some distance from where the bomb landed. We crowded around. It was a gruesome sight; his gray, dust-covered body was littered with shrapnel wounds, his mouth gaping, a large piece of flesh hung from his forehead exposing his skull, and his neck was contorted, broken, with his limbs sprawled at awkward angles, blood pooling from beneath his head. His hand still clutched the now-empty bucket, bent out of place by rocks.

The gruesome image was seared into my brain. Seconds before, he'd been alive and well, my friend from the orphanage. Death had come so quickly. The same could happen to us at any given moment.

Shant stood up, "Help residents put out the fires. And bandage the wounded. Levon cannot be helped."

He spoke with deep regret. Perhaps he blamed himself for the death. I could see that Raffi had been struck silent, staring at the corpse. At this point I was no less traumatized than he was. Death was all around us now. But, we had a job. It was something that could at least get our minds off of this tragedy. I turned my attention to the house across the street. One wall of the house had crumbled, exposing the inside, and a woman had run out through the door with a bucket of her own. Citizens were stockpiling their own water for drinking, it was a pity when it needed to be used on a fire.

I took Raffi's hand, and forced him to walk with me, away from Levon.

"Thank goodness. Are there more of you?" she asked, throwing water on the burning garden, and trying to stamp the fire out. Though her walls were brick the fire could spread to her roof or inside her house.

"There are, but we lost our bucket," I said.

She looked dismayed, and darted back into her house for some more water.

"What do we do now?" Raffi asked, finally speaking.

"We'll stay here and see if the lady wants more help from us," I said, "I hope the other scouts in charge of fighting fires get here soon."

Soon the rest of the kids were told to scour the neighborhood and find anyone willing to help put out the blaze. We were joined by women and children; they had been hiding away in their homes while the men fought with the resistance. By the time the Boy Scout troop in charge of firefighting arrived with water and hoses the fires were largely contained, and night had fallen.

In a show of gratitude we were invited into the home of a woman whose home we'd saved from the flames. Her husband had gone off to fight and she was childless.

"Make yourselves at home," she insisted, handing us bread to eat. She gave us all the bread she had left. Even though Shant told her she shouldn't have, she said that everyone would have as much food as they needed when the Russians came, and they would come soon. We had so little to eat, our food was rationed and we wouldn't be getting more of it with the Ottoman soldiers and their stranglehold on the city. I myself was becoming more malnourished because I was looking out for Raffi, giving him a portion of my food. How I missed the orphanage food then. Now I knew why we were always told to be grateful for what was on our plate even if we were quite tired of eating the same old thing over and over. How fortunate Fimi was to be able to stay there, I thought. We'd heard that the girls had been put to work making uniforms and food for the fighters, as well as for us, which was delivered to Dr. Ussher's Mission. I missed Fimi a lot, the more I thought about her. What was she doing right now? She was probably very worried about Raffi and me.

Raffi and I tried never to speak of Levon again, lest it conjure the images of his death in our minds once more. There would be time to mourn when the siege was over. Avoiding thoughts of Levon's death became like avoiding staring at the sun; to look directly at it was painful, yet it colored everything we saw.

Zangi

In the ensuing days of the siege the gunshots and bombs which filled the air were not so constant; the Turkish troops had decided to strike with more precision and save their ammo. This was almost more nerve-wrecking; the harsh blasts would come suddenly and out of nowhere now. There was a marching band that circulated the city to help alleviate this; musicians unable to fight instead tried to boost our morale by playing traditional Armenian songs in a nonstop parade. Raffi would be smiling and clapping to the music whenever they passed us. After days of bombardment, the bullets which hadn't killed anyone were extracted by the thousands and recast to be used by our soldiers. They were easy to find. Our troop had uncovered hundreds already. It was prideful but unnerving work; if bullets flew here once they could do so again without warning. We made the work more interesting by turning it into a sort of game. Whoever found the most casings won. There was no real prize, just bragging rights.

On the afternoon of the 26th of April, while we were crouched on the ground sifting through gravel and rubble for used bullets, we heard a whimpering noise come from behind a nearby building, and were approached by a half-starved dog, whose owner had either died or abandoned it by now.

"Hey Vartan, look! A dog!"

Raffi instantly forgot his work and went to meet the dog, petting it. It was as tall as his chest, and dark brown.

"Are you lost?" he asked it, as if it could answer, "Where is your owner?"

"Come back here," I called to Raffi, not wanting him to wander off, "Now's not exactly the time for finding a new pet."

While marching through the city we'd seen stray animals before. Every time we caught sight of a cat Raffi would shout "Kitty!!" and want to chase after it, but these shell-shocked cats would have none of it. This was the first dog we'd come into contact with though.

"But he's lost and hungry," Raffi insisted, "We've helped people who are lost and hungry, why not dogs too?"

"Because they're animals."

"But don't you remember the story about the boy who found two puppies, and when they grew up they protected him from dragons?"

"Zangi and Zarangi, yes," I remembered the story well, one I had told Raffi back at the orphanage not long ago. The young hero had enlisted the help of his two dogs to liberate a kingdom from a group of dragons, which had conquered the kingdom by stealing the eyes of its citizens; the boy tricked the dragons into letting them tie their mane around a tree only for the dogs to consume them whole afterward, "That was just a story. Things like that don't really happen. Now leave it be, I don't want you to get fleas."

"If we show this dog kindness, he can protect us," Raffi said, hugging the dog, oblivious to my warning about fleas, "I think I'll name him Zangi. We'll need another one so that we can name it Zarangi."

"You won't name him anything," I ordered, "Come back here Raffi, and help us find bullets."

"What's going on here?" Shant asked with commanding authority. He spotted the dog.

"I'm sorry Shant, Raffi saw the dog stagger out from behind the building and he went up to it."

Shant walked up to the dog, and looked at Raffi as if to silently demand an explanation.

"I thought maybe he could help us," Raffi said.

Shant was silent for a moment, in thought. An explosion rocked the other side of the city during his pause, but no one even flinched. It was far, after all.

"He can help us."

"Really?" Raffi asked in surprise.

"You two go take the dog to the Mission and hand it over to the man awaiting our bullets. He will know what to do with it. You'll find out how he can help us tonight."

"Alright!" Raffi said happily.

Using some spare rope from our supplies Shant fashioned a leash for the dog, and handed it to Raffi.

"Be careful out there," he said to me, "The Mission isn't far from here. Stay there for the time being and I'll come get you later."

I agreed, and the two of us departed from the rest of the group, heading down the narrow, crooked and abandoned streets of

Aigestan toward Dr. Ussher's Mission. Raffi had a huge smile on his face the entire time, but I had a feeling Shant had plans for that dog that Raffi wasn't going to like. We were low on food supplies, after all. But I didn't know for sure what he was going to have us do with the dog.

Raffi meanwhile, was becoming increasingly attached to the dog; something I knew in my gut was unwise. The dog was quite tame, even though we were strangers. I briefly wondered what this dog's story was.

"We need to find him something to eat," said Raffi, "I bet he's hungry."

"There's hardly enough food to go around for humans. I don't know where we'll find any."

"Hm," Raffi looked around with a worried expression, but there was nothing along the street but dirt and rubble.

"They'll find something for him to eat when we get to the Mission," I said, hoping to make Raffi feel better.

Raffi knelt down and picked up a stick lying in the street, allowing the dog to sniff it.

"Catch it, Zangi!" he exclaimed, throwing the stick and letting go of the leash.

"Raffi, what are you doing?!" I exclaimed, thinking the dog would escape.

But, my worries were put to rest when the dog picked the stick up in its mouth, and trotted over to Raffi with it. Raffi petted the dog's head.

"Good dog, Zangi," he cooed.

"You're too much, you know that? Will you hold onto the leash until we get to the Mission? Or should I do it myself?"

"Oh alright," Raffi sighed, "You're no fun sometimes, Vartan."

"This isn't a time for fun. If I didn't take charge of you and just let you do whatever you want to do we'd have both already been blown up by a bomb or shot by now."

Raffi grumbled to himself, keeping the leash tight in his hand. We occasionally had our differences. Sometimes, especially since the siege started, I felt less like his big brother and more like his parent. Perhaps at age eight I too would have disregarded the bombs detonating around me and played fetch with a stray dog. But I knew I couldn't be that way anymore, for both our sakes. Raffi still had something that I had lost somewhere along the way. I was glad this siege and all of the death he had witnessed hadn't killed that innocence in him yet.

When we got to the gates of the Mission, an old man was waiting where Shant said he would be, to take the used bullet casings we found and deliver them to someone who would cast new bullets out of them. He wore a fur cap and a long coat, his arm in a sling. He was dressed in the garb of an Armenian fedayi fighter, but was too old or too injured to join the fight. Perhaps he had been injured fighting.

"Did Shant send you?" he asked.

"Yes, the rest of the troop is still looking for used bullets," I explained.

"We found this dog, mister," Raffi said, "Shant said to bring it to you. Do you know where we can find some food for it?"

The soldier eyed the dog, before patting its head.

"It seems friendly. Good find, boys. Give me the leash."

"What are you going to do?" Raffi asked.

"I'll take it somewhere where it will be fed and looked after. You'll see it later. Perhaps tonight, if Shant wants to take you."

Raffi looked down at his new dog, a sense of worry in his voice.

"Well, okay. Zangi, go with this man now, he's going to find you some food," Raffi said, stroking the dog.

The soldier took the leash.

"Wait here for the rest of your group to return," He instructed, "It is too dangerous to roam about the city by yourselves, for any length of time."

"Understood, sir," I said.

The man was off, taking the dog with him.

"I hope Zangi will be okay without us for a while," Raffi said.

"He will be," I said, and we sat on the ground.

At the edge of neutral ground, I felt safer waiting here. I knew the Turkish army wouldn't shoot in this direction. Instead of gunshots, however, the distant sound of wailing met our ears. Looking down the street to the left we saw another Boy Scout troop, heading toward the hospital with a stretcher. This was a job we hadn't been given yet at this point. They were carrying a woman with them. Raffi and I got to our feet as they reached the gate.

"Hurry! We're almost there!" shouted the boy in front.

The woman's belly was bloated and she was screaming. She was pregnant. And this was an awful time to be giving birth. Her screams were loud and piercing, making me wonder if perhaps something else was wrong too. But I couldn't tell.

"What's wrong with her?" Raffi asked in concern as they brought her through the hospital gates.

"I think she's having a baby," I replied.

"Is it going to be our turn to carry injured people to the hospital tomorrow?"

"I don't know when we'll be doing that."

"It's going to be scary…" Raffi hugged his sides, "I don't want to."

"We'll have to do as Shant says. Someone has to do that job."

"Why does it have to be us?" Raffi asked.

"I don't think anyone in the city is just doing nothing. We will lose the battle if we don't do anything. We all have our jobs."

A short time later, Shant returned with our group, we watched them approach from a distance with a bag full of used bullet casings.

"Did you hand the dog to the man here?" Shant asked.

"Yes sir, he left with it some time ago," I answered.

"Then we wait."

"Shant," Raffi said, "Can you take us to see the dog tonight?"

"Do you really want to see that?" Shant asked.

Raffi nodded, "The man said maybe you would let us see the dog tonight."

"Ahh…" Shant seemed to have realized something, but we didn't know what, "If you are certain that you want to see the dog tonight, I will bring you with me. You may learn something."

Raffi smiled and cheered, but I had a feeling he didn't know what he was getting himself into.

We waited for a few more minutes before the old man returned for the bullets, and then we were off to scavenge for more elsewhere. That night we stayed at the Mission, sleeping on the ground in the lobby. Though the Mission was the safest place in the city, we had to suffer hearing the screams and wails of injured patients. In the early days of the siege most of the patients were there for shrapnel or bullet wounds, but a few were surviving victims of torture that the Turkish soldiers had left at the gates of the city as a message. As we set up camp on the ground with spare blankets and pillows given to us by the hospital, Shant approached Raffi.

"Are you ready? The operation leaves now."

"Yes!" Raffi said with enthusiasm.

"Does your friend want to come with?"

"I think I'd better," I replied.

"Very good, follow me then," he said, before getting other boys to join the night mission.

Shant took Raffi, me, and three other boys to a burned down building behind Tabriz Gate, accompanied by a fedayi fighter, armed with his rifle. Tabriz Gate, so named because it faced in the direction of the Iranian city of Tabriz, was a gateway in the stone walls surrounding the city, leading out to an open field that stretched toward the Varak Mountains in the East, where brigades of Ottoman soldiers sat in trenches, waiting. This was the main entrance to the city. It was a small distance from the Mission, but far enough to where the danger of being shot or bombed was significantly higher here. Scores of dead bodies lined the streets, or laid in the gateway in their own blood. The smell was overwhelmingly putrid. Many of the bodies outside of the walls had been butchered and mutilated, left there by the Turks as a preview of what they would do should they make it past the walls of the city. Buildings near the gate were crumbling and craters left from cannons were everywhere. It was a piece of Hell on Earth. We hid behind the remains of a stone wall for cover, with the stray dog we had found earlier in the day in tow.

"What are we bringing the dog here for?" Raffi asked.

"Raffi, I want you to tie this lantern to the dog's neck," Shant said, handing me a lantern and a rope to give to Raffi before looking around the edge of the wall to make sure it was clear.

I gave the lantern and rope to Raffi, "Do as Shant says."

"It's so he can see better in the dark, yes?" Raffi asked, using his knot-tying knowledge to tie the lantern around the makeshift collar that Zangi was wearing, both he and the dog trusting Shant, who didn't bother to answer Raffi's question, focusing on his view around the wall at the gate.

The Turkish army was stationed just outside the city walls. The gates were guarded by Armenian gunmen hiding on rooftops and atop the wall itself; it was one spot where they had reached a stalemate. Jevdet Bey's tactic was to shoot anybody who tried to leave, in case we tried to escape towards enemy lines. There was talk of sending for help from the Russians, but it would be a suicide mission. Someone would need a way to get past the Turkish army.

The dog was about as high as my waist. It looked up at me with big black eyes. Raffi finished fitting the lantern around the dog's neck. By now, I could chance a guess at what Shant was going to do with the dog, and though I didn't like it, I knew it was necessary. It wasn't going to be pretty though. Raffi looked on, still innocent and unaware. I knew it was cruel not to tell Raffi what was going to be done to the dog. I wished he had stayed behind at the Mission because this was not the sort of thing I wanted him to have to witness. The three other boys with us looked somber as well. I think they knew what was about to happen. They were closer to my age and from our orphanage, the sons of slaughtered Armenians from the villages. New orphans were coming in droves to the city, and the few boys among those orphans, lucky enough to survive slaughter in one way or another, were transferred straight from Sporri's orphanage to the Boy Scout troops.

Shant looked back at Raffi, "Good, Raffi. You're a good soldier. I am about to give you a lesson in sacrifice. Let me explain this to you before I do so, so that you understand. The Turks have weapons, and those weapons have bullets. Each bullet in those guns would kill an Armenian if they had it their way. So each bullet they waste is a bullet that does not kill an Armenian. Do you understand me so far, boy?"

Raffi nodded slowly. I could see that he was starting to hyperventilate.

"We need to make them waste more bullets. Zangi is going to help us with that. I told you he could help us against the Turks, didn't I?"

"Y-you did sir."

"Your dog is going to be a hero. Now as for the rest of you, I want you all to stay behind the wall, duck down low, and be ready to flee when I say so. You'll be covered by our friend here. Now stay back."

Shant then took the dog by the rope and walked it to the gate. Raffi and I peeked around the corner. Shant kicked Zangi, and the dog yelped loudly and ran out of the gate and into the open field. The next thing we heard were hundreds of guns going off at the poor creature, the soldiers thinking they were shooting at an Armenian. Then we heard more distant gun shots, shot by Turkish soldiers that thought the Russians were attacking on the other side of the city. Guns were going off around the whole perimeter of Aigestan. Raffi gripped me tightly as we both ducked, and sobbed into my chest. Every bullet that hit that dog was a bullet that would not hit us. This was what we had to keep in mind.

Mission

As the siege which had begun in April slowly bled into May, the hospital at the American Mission became a place of horror and woe, filled with the groans and screams of the injured, hungry, diseased and dying. Raffi and I bore witness to the city becoming more and more crowded, filling up with more refugees than we could take care of. This was according to Jevdet Bey's plan; counter-intuitive as it may have at first seemed, the Turkish army was actually allowing Armenian refugees from nearby, ransacked villages in the countryside safe passage into the city. The plan was to starve us out. And rather than risk staying in other, more dangerous parts of the city, as many refugees as could possibly fit pushed their way into the hospital daily, due in part to the fact that the Ottoman army wasn't allowed to shoot at an American building. But they weren't supposed to stay unless injured or severely starved. It was in this bloody place that our group took a turn doing daily shift, on the 1st of May.

Shant led Raffi and I with five other boys to the gates of the hospital early that morning from the church we had spent the night at. We didn't know what we were going to be put to work doing, but I dreaded having to actually go into the hospital. Shant contended that his hand was feeling better, and his higher-ups apparently must have agreed. He was carrying a rifle with him today. We knew though that whenever someone got a firearm they didn't have before, it was because a fedayi fighter had died.

"I am not allowed to enter with my gun," he said, motioning to the rifle strapped over his shoulder, "You go on ahead, Dr. Ussher will tell you what you need to do. I will be back to get you at sundown."

Raffi clung to my arm tightly and watched in disbelief as Shant walked away, back down the street. I knew how he felt, this sudden abandonment by the only adult we had looking after us was jarring, though I understood why Shant had left us here. The other boys stared down the road too, uneager to part with the security he'd provided us.

"He's not supposed to leave us. Where is he going?" Raffi asked, looking up at me with pleading eyes.

"I think there's a rule about not having weapons here," I said, "But no one's going to hurt us here."

"Why can't he just leave his gun outside?" asked the bandaged Vatche, who was on the verge of panicking without our shepherd around to guide us.

"They probably need him on Castle Rock today," I said.

It was safe to assume that was where he would be going, if he had been given a gun. But if he was a soldier now, was he still going to be guiding our Boy Scout troop? Or would we have another injured soldier guiding us? Though a harsh leader, especially over the Zangi ordeal, I'd come to feel comforted by his presence. I think that Raffi did too, to a degree.

Raffi hadn't been quite the same since the night we were forced to send Zangi to his untimely demise. His tears had lasted the rest of the night until he fell asleep, and in the last three days he'd lost most of his cheer, and had become fearful and clung even more tightly to me, if that were possible. I suppose, after suppressing the memory of Levon's death, having to play a role in his new 'pet' being shot to death had finally shown him the reality of our situation, as much as I hated to see that happen to him. But he had to mature to survive now.

The rattling sound of distant gunfire filled the air just then, frightening us without the presence of Shant. At once feeling very vulnerable, we all then rushed through the gate, pushing and shoving, eager to get into neutral territory where, if not completely diminished, the threat to our lives was much lower.

The front lawn was filled with people camping out for safety on its grounds, most of them wounded and wearing bloodied bandages, slings and casts, others half-starved, some wearing only hospital gowns, having nothing else on their backs. And these were just the people who were well enough not to need to be inside. They were mainly women and children, refugees from other villages that were wounded before fleeing as their homes were pillaged and torched. From the stories going around, men rarely made it as far as Van before they were put to death.

"Where do we go now?" asked Hrant.

"I think we're supposed to go inside the hospital," Vatche replied, "Maybe Ussher is going to give us something to do."

"We'll be lucky if we don't get typhus in there," said Hrant.

"Let's see what they need us to do," I said, reluctantly taking the lead.

We had to step over some of the people crowding outside the hospital to get to the entrance. The inside of the building, however, was even worse. We were met with a sickening stench the moment we walked in, the stench of disease, rotting flesh and death. Fear returned to our hearts. One of the orderlies saw us walk in and approached us.

"Are you the Boy Scouts sent to help us today?"

We nodded. Raffi was holding his nose.

"Come with me, I'll find Dr. Ussher and ask him what he wants to have you do today."

We were going to be led deeper into the hospital. I feared not only for Raffi but for myself, having to witness firsthand what was being done to Armenians by Turkish soldiers and Kurdish marauders outside of the city. We had been lucky enough to mostly avoid it thus far. The nurse led us through the door and past a series of hospital beds, many with blood-soaked blankets, containing people who shrieked and moaned, or else lay silent as if dead. The wounds people received at the hands of the Turks were sickening. I do not wish to think about how mutilated some people were, either from bullets or shrapnel, or if they were unlucky enough, a sword. To this day, seared deep into my psyche are images of a man whose nose had been cut off, another missing his ears, a woman with burns on her face and arms in the shape of a branding iron meant for cattle, people with missing fingers or limbs. This was what Hell must look like. All of us were struck with horror. It had become pointless to shield Raffi's eyes. I wished someone were there to shield my eyes.

Where was my father in all of this madness, I wondered? Would he ever make it back to Van? Was he...going to have this done to him too? I clasped Raffi's hand tightly, trying to hold back my tears and stave off the panic in my heart. This place was terrifying.

It was remarkable that the hospital was so full. One had to admire Dr. Clarence Ussher's willingness to care for all of these people, the majority of them from outside the city. He wasn't obligated to do so, to my knowledge. But to make matters worse for the hospital, typhus fever was spreading through the city. If someone didn't have a horrific wound, they were in the hospital for that. Those suffering from illness were being kept in a different wing. There was not a vacant bed left in the whole hospital; those who didn't need to be in a bed anymore were outside on the lawn.

Dr. Clarence Ussher was busy bandaging a man's feet when we found him. The man, bearded, dressed in peasant rags and perhaps in his forties, panted with ragged hoarseness, with closed, teary eyes. Lying atop the table beside the man's bed next to Dr. Ussher's pliers were around six bloody nails, and two horseshoes. The signature punishment of Jevdet Bey. I don't know if Raffi was able to piece everything together, but the sight of it chilled me to the core.

Dr. Ussher regarded us with a greeting in English, turning to his nurse and speaking to her. She nodded to him, and then turned to us.

"Dr. Ussher welcomes you," the nurse said to us in Armenian, "There is much work to be done around here and he is grateful for your help."

Dr. Ussher, his voice comforting and fatherly to my ears, said something else to the nurse, who then translated for us once more.

"Our patients need to have food brought to them. You may start by taking milk, eggs and bread from the kitchen, and handing it to patients both inside the hospital and in the courtyard."

That sounded fair enough. At least we weren't going to be stitching people's wounds or the like. But it still meant we had to be confronted with the butchery going on outside Van.

"But remember," the nurse added, without Dr. Ussher having told her anything further, "Only give one meal per person. Our rations are limited. Don't let anyone talk you into giving more than their share, and don't take any for yourselves. You will be fed at noon. And the milk is only for babies. Our nurses will be providing water for everyone else."

Dr. Ussher asked her something and she replied, telling him what she'd told us. He then said something else, and then looked at us.

"Did you understand everything?" the nurse asked.

I gave an obedient nod, others responded 'yes'.

The nurse gave a small smile, and continued in Armenian, "Good, these rules are very important, please do not break them. Now then, come with me, I will bring you to where you can get the food."

The nurse then led us from that room down the hall toward a kitchen, run by other nurses who no doubt had not anticipated that they would be caring for so many people when they first became missionaries. Here the nurses sanitized bottles and filled them with milk to give to us, placing rubber nipples on each, along with also handing us loaves of bread and hard boiled eggs. We were each given a basket and told to go our separate ways and disperse the food as quickly as possible, and to return to the kitchen when the baskets were empty. It was probably a mistake to hand food out to boys who were already so hungry; I heard later a couple of the boys got in trouble for eating the food out of their own basket.

Each of us went in different directions, that is of course except for Raffi, my shadow, who trailed close behind me as I stepped over people's legs down the hallway and made my way toward the doors to the outside. I couldn't wait to get outside. I had to get away from it all. The other boys would have followed me outside, none of them wanted to be stuck inside the hospital with the stench and the horror, but the nurse saw me walk that way first so I got to be the one to work outside. But somehow, she didn't stop Raffi.

"I think we're supposed to split up, Raffi," I said, a bit annoyed.

"But I want to go with you," he replied, on the cusp of whining if I pressed the issue further, "I don't want to be by myself here. I want to go outside."

"We will be able to feed more people if we go our own ways," I explained, "That is why the nurse wanted us to do that."

"I'll feed the people right next to the ones you feed. Come on, please? I'll be good, I promise."

Twenty four hours a day he needed to be right by my side. Only when using a toilet was I allowed a moment to myself. It was okay if we were out in the city where it was dangerous, but here, where we were relatively safe? Never have I known a more emotionally dependent child. And it wasn't even the siege causing it either. He'd always been this way. I had not a solitary moment to myself since he joined the orphanage! Keeping these gripes to myself, I relented, while simultaneously cursing myself for being so nice all the time.

"Alright, Raffi, but you need to do your part too," I said, opening the doors, "You help the person right next to the one I'm helping, and we will finish twice as fast."

Raffi gave a nod and smiled as I walked through and approached a ragged woman and her two young children sitting on the front steps. Their faces were all darkened by the blistering sun, and the mother had a bandage over one eye. The children, both younger than Raffi, smiled brightly when they saw what was in our baskets, having probably not eaten in a long time, however long it would have taken them to safely travel from their village to Van. By the look of them, I could chance to guess it had taken them a few days. I handed the mother some food, which she gladly took and ate greedily, as the children clamored over Raffi's basket.

"Only one each," Raffi tried to tell them, but they didn't listen.

Their mother swatted her children's wrists away and took their rations herself. As she did, I noticed her take four eggs when she only needed three. Something stopped me from calling her out on it. Perhaps it was pity.

"Sorry, they're just hungry," the mother said, handing them bread and an egg each, discreetly hiding the other egg in a pocket.

"Oh, that's alright," Raffi said, looking to me as I moved to the next patient, "Wait for me Vartan."

"There's no time to wait," I replied, giving bread and an egg to a young girl sitting on the steps of the stairs.

Raffi was determined to keep up, quickly going to the next person and giving them their rations. As we put some distance between ourselves and the first patients we helped, I stopped Raffi.

"Listen Raffi; don't let them take the food from the basket themselves. Hand the food to them and move on."

"But why?" Raffi asked.

"You may not have noticed, but they might take more food from your basket than they are supposed to. I saw it happen with the first lady we helped, she grabbed an extra egg."

"Really? That's cheating!"

"Just watch what they take from now on," I said, and I moved on, handing food to the next person.

We worked out way through the courtyard. Two nurses soon came out from the hospital with water rations for the people we'd already gotten to. The water had to be drawn from a well outside, which was why we weren't distributing water as well, having come from the kitchen. Perhaps that would be another job for later. We were a good distance ahead of the nurses though; people would have to wait to get water with their meals.

Most of the patients were respectful and didn't try to bargain for more of their fair share. There were some who did anyway, however.

"Young boy, my children and I are half-starved," pleaded one mother to Raffi, with one child who looked to be about three, another merely an infant, "Might we have more food? We need it."

Raffi hesitated, looking over to me.

"We aren't supposed to," I said, handing milk to a mother for her baby, "We don't have enough."

"This ration isn't enough for me," the mother insisted, "It isn't enough for my children either."

"I'm sorry Miss," Raffi said, both hands on the handle of the basket as he shrunk back, away from her grasp.

"No one will have to know, child."

"But I'm not supposed to…"

"Come on, Raffi," I said, finally interjecting and taking him by the arm.

"Wicked child! May the roof fall on your head!" the mother yelled, shouting more curses as I pulled Raffi away, but, her baby began to scream, and rather than continue she took to comforting it with a milk bottle.

"Vartan, what am I supposed to do when they want more?" Raffi asked, "Isn't it mean to say no to them?"

"If you give someone more than they're supposed to get, then that means there will be someone else who doesn't get any at all," I explained, "That's even meaner, right?"

"I guess so…"

"Now keep at it," I said, patting his back and moving toward the next needy patient, "You can handle this job. You can't expect me to be there to rescue you all the time."

Collecting used bullet shells, helping to reinforce houses and putting out fires had all been done in groups, Raffi had always had me to lean on throughout all these. This job was different from the others.

The two of us continued making rounds through the paved path in the courtyard to the gates until our baskets became low. Giving the last of my rations to a lone child, I watched Raffi as came to another single mother nearby, one who looked absolutely famished, cradling a newborn infant wrapped in a blanket in her arms. Raffi gave her a slice of bread, but she had her arms too full to take an egg, let alone a milk bottle.

"Son, the Turkish gendarmes marched me fifty kilometers to come here, with not a thing to eat besides grass in the fields and whatever I could find crawling on the ground. I cannot even make milk for my baby. If you could, please, would one of you take my baby so that I can have a few moments to eat?"

"But I have to get back to the kitchen for more food to give to people," Raffi said, "My friend Vartan said that I have to move quickly so that everyone gets some food."

"I need help from someone."

"Raffi, go ahead and help her," I said, "I'll take your basket and go get it refilled in the meantime."

Raffi looked worried, "But I've never even held a baby before. What if I do something wrong?"

"You'll do fine," I said, taking his basket from him, "The baby's mother will show you what to do."

"Thank you, dear boy," the mother said, "Here, sit down."

I watched as Raffi sat on the ground cross-legged, and the mother carefully placed the baby in his arms. By the look on his face you'd think someone had placed a bomb in his lap that could explode unexpectedly at any given moment. He looked too afraid to even flinch the wrong way and hurt the baby.

Entrusting the job to him, I headed back inside, through the crowded hallways and back toward the kitchen. When I returned there, the nursemaids were busy rolling dough for the bread.

"Why do you have two baskets?" one asked.

"My friend is helping a mother care for a baby while she eats." I asked, "We'll get going again once I bring his basket back."

The nurse smiled, "Herr Sporri has done a great job with you kids. You'll see, this war will end soon enough, when the Russians come to liberate us, and you and your friends will be upstanding young men when it finishes."

She filled our baskets up with bread, eggs and milk.

"You can carry all that, right?"

I nodded, "I can carry this."

"Alright, strong one, I'll see you when you return."

It was a heavy load, but I made my trek back down the hallway, stepping over people and avoiding collisions. I opened the door by pushing my shoulder into it. Scanning the area, I found Raffi and the young mother. She was showing Raffi how to feed a baby with a bottle.

"How are you holding up?" I asked Raffi as I approached him, he diligently concentrating on the task at hand.

"I think I'm getting it…" he said, not taking his eyes off the baby for fear of making one wrong move.

The mother smiled, eating her meager rations, "He's been a great help. I don't know where this hospital would be without you boys."

"We do our best, " I placed Raffi's basket down beside him, "I'm going to feed more people. You can continue once this mother is done eating. But don't take too long."

Raffi nodded and I continued on handing out rations to the needy patients. For the first time, I felt proud of him.

Raffi

Food supplies were growing shorter. Jevdet Bey's strategy of giving us more mouths to feed was taking its toll. Though the Armenians had become particularly effective in getting the Ottoman army to waste its ammunition, their army had legitimate means of replenishing it; the Armenians had to make their own. Fires raged uncontrollably outside Aigestan, it was beyond our ability to fight them. When one could catch sight of the rest of the city from over the walls it seemed like it had been hit by a tornado, or ravaged by God like Sodom and Gomorrah. It wasn't Van anymore. Even if we survived this siege and Van became a part of Russia, how could it ever be the same again? I didn't think it ever would be.

It was May 4th when our troop finally drew the short straw and was assigned the most nauseating, mind-scarring job we could get, as assistants in the hospital, helping to tend to the wounded. It had to happen sometime. I was hoping the siege would end before we got this job, but it showed no signs of ending. When the siege first started I imagined it would go on for two, maybe three days. What a fool I was.

But, it wasn't as if our troop didn't have the knowledge needed to aid the patients. We knew how to splint a broken arm, apply bandages, resuscitate those who'd stopped breathing. Girls from the orphanages were now being called upon for these kinds of jobs as well, although most were still in charge of sewing and stitching clothes for the fighters. I hoped I may run into Fimi again sometime. It would have done me good to see her face again, something pretty for me to behold after almost two weeks of ugliness. I didn't realize that I would be seeing her again, much sooner than I had expected.

Raffi had grown much in such a short time. When we were at the hospital and not out in the city where it was dangerous, more and more he showed himself capable of doing his tasks independently, without my constant guidance. At the same time, I don't think he was the same boy he used to be. As if the siege had broken him inside. He was more silent, contemplative, less likely to laugh and giggle at any little distraction. Less likely to go after stray animals, or listen in amazement to my stories, to take them for face value. I continued to tell him a little more about Davit of Sasun or the vishap dragons on Mt. Vasak, but he simply listened silently now. Maybe the old Raffi would come back after the siege. Maybe he wouldn't. We were both growing up too fast.

We began the day by helping to move wounded patients into other parts of the hospital with a stretcher. This was a job I couldn't do with Raffi because of our height difference, so we were paired with boys around our own height. Armen was only a year younger than I, and close enough to my height so that the two of us were put in charge of transferring children to other beds or wings in the hospital. We did this until lunch time (a fine meal of either donkey or cat meat with some stale bread; supplies were diminishing quickly), after which time we were given other jobs.

As fate would have it, after lunch that day Raffi and I were paired with Dr. Clarence Ussher himself as he went from bed to bed, tirelessly doing all that he could to help the growing number of patients. One such patient was a little girl, with a shaven head. At once, I recognized her.

"Fimi!" I exclaimed.

"You know this girl?" Dr. Ussher asked, in Armenian.

In the past few months, and especially during the siege, Dr. Ussher had evidently picked up some Armenian language, having to deal with an untold number of Armenian patients each day since the refugees entered the city.

"She's our friend," Raffi said, looking over her bedside.

Fimi was covered in cuts and bruises, many of them deep and bleeding. Shrapnel had embedded itself in her skin.

Fimi turned to us, "Raffi...Vartan, is that you?"

"What happened?" I asked.

"They were taking us to the church with the other girls, "she muttered weakly, "And then, there was an explosion. I broke my arm."

A cannon blast. I could see the signs on her body now. I was just happy that she was alive.

"You're lucky, poor Levon died that same way," said Raffi.

"Levon is dead?" Fimi asked, surprised and concerned.

"Afraid so," I said, "A bomb exploded right next to him."

"That's terrible! I...I can't believe it."

"Raffi and I are going to help you," I assured her, "That's our job today. We're with Dr. Ussher."

Raffi stayed at my side, as we assisted Dr. Ussher at Fimi's bedside. We were tasked with handing him medical tools from a metal tray, and bandaging her wounds after pieces of wood and metal were removed. Before beginning, Dr. Ussher and his nurses walked us through what each tool was called in English, so that when he called for a tool we knew which one he meant. It made things easier for him if we learned what he called each tool. Unfortunately, the hospital was out of sedatives; Fimi needed to be strapped to the bed. Fimi would whimper, cry and scream throughout the procedure.

"She's going to live, right?" Raffi asked me.

"Her wounds aren't too serious," I assured him.

The shrapnel would need to be removed before we could put a splint on her arm, and there was a large splinter in her bicep which would need special attention. From what I understood, Dr. Ussher didn't want it to bleed out too much after he removed it.

"Tourniquet," Dr. Ussher said.

Raffi gave him a long leather strap to wrap around Fimi's arm.

"You'll be alright," Raffi said, to comfort Fimi, "Vartan said your wounds aren't too serious."

Fimi nodded, but said nothing. She gritted her teeth and tried to get through the pain. She wanted to tough it out.

"The tweezers," Dr. Ussher requested.

Strange word, "tweezers". I still remember that word. But I knew what he meant. I handed them to the doctor; it seemed now that Raffi's job had become moral support for Fimi. Raffi and I both had taken a fancy to her at the orphanage I think, Raffi in his own childish way, though neither of us were ready to admit it. She had been a tomboy beneath those forced feminine coverings, and though we were divided often by gender in the orphanage, she would spend time with us whenever she could. Strange that we should meet again, like this.

Fimi braced herself as he carefully removed the splinter that jutted out of her arm. As he slowly pulled it out, she screamed, and blood flowed from the wound. Raffi let Fimi squeeze his hand. Once it was over, Dr. Ussher poured some peroxide over the wound and cleaned it, making Raffi wince as it sizzled and garnering even more shrieks from Fimi.

"Suture, and needle," Dr. Ussher said finally.

I handed him the materials, and the doctor expertly stitched the bleeding wound. Despite herself, Fimi sniffled and cried. And there was much more to be removed. We were with her for several hours, until the sun went down, getting every piece of shrapnel out of her until Ussher was ready to put her arm in a splint.

It was then that Shant approached the hospital bed. We'd been seeing less and less of him lately, but he had brought us to the hospital today.

"Dr. Ussher, we need help at the tents," Shant said, "We have three men, wounded by gunshot. We are out of medical supplies, but with your help we might be able to save them. I need to stay with the other boys today, so I cannot bring them myself."

Though Dr. Ussher could not treat the fighters of the resistance at his hospital, and only officially treated civilians caught in the crossfire of the siege, he had been lending the fighters medical supplies. He could not personally go to their tents to bring them their supplies either. Though it was unlikely the Turks would ever find out about it, doing anything to raise their ire was a risk he did not want to take. If Jevdet Bey ever heard even a shred of credible evidence about his providing direct aid to these supposed enemies of the Ottoman Empire, he would have an excuse to bomb the Mission. I presume the only thing that kept him from doing so was diplomatic red tape.

A nursemaid translated Shant's message to Dr. Ussher. He paused for a moment, sighing and taking a handkerchief from his coat to wipe himself. This job seemed to be taking a lot out of the man.

"I will send someone from here to the tents to deliver the supplies," said Dr. Ussher, in his best Armenian, "Let me know exactly how much you need, and I will have one of my nurses get them together for you."

Shant discussed the amount of bandages, sutures and other supplies with Dr. Ussher, with the aid of a translator. The nursemaid was there to clear up any misunderstandings.

"Perhaps we can have one of the boys here deliver the supplies," Shant suggested.

"That may be the best course of action," said Dr. Ussher, "Send one of the older boys."

"We may need someone to help us with some small tasks and chores at the front as well if we have any volunteers," said Shant, "They're stationed on Castle Rock near the old fortress."

"Take whoever seems the most fit and the fastest. It is a most dangerous mission."

His translator reiterated the message to Shant in Armenian.

Shant looked around, seeing no other boys in the room, before his eyes came to rest on me.

"Vartan, how would you like to deliver the supplies and help out at Castle Rock? You must be quick, and you must be quiet. Never walk out in the open. You cannot risk being seen by the enemy for even an instant. Nightfall is soon, perhaps I will have someone send another dog out to keep the Turks busy while you help transport the wounded to the tents. After that, you may return to the hospital."

I stood frozen. Out of everyone he could have chosen, he had chosen me. It was an uneasy honor to say the least. I didn't know what it would be like being right where the fighters were. But I trusted Shant, and I wanted to be of help. But then I felt Raffi tug on my arm.

"Vartan, I don't want you to leave me," he said.

I looked at him and then at Shant.

"Raffi should stay here," Shant said.

"Raffi, I have to agree," I said, "You can stay here and keep Fimi company. I will be back tonight."

"You said you wouldn't leave me! " Raffi yelled, "Either you stay or I will come with you."

"No Raffi... you stay here where it is safe. I promise I will come back safely," I said, making up my mind.

I had to go back on my promise to stay by his side throughout the siege, just this once. I was determined to make it through this alive and come back to Raffi and Fimi.

"After this I will not leave your side again if I can help it," I said.

Raffi gave a sigh and looked down. He hated being alone, I could see it. We both hated to be alone. That was how we became brothers. I may not have always enjoyed taking care of him all the time, but I would have been much worse off without any friend at all. I lifted his chin up.

"I will come back to you, Raffi. I will promise you this."

"Promise me too," said Fimi.

I nodded to her, "You too Fimi. I hope that you recover well. Raffi will take care of you."

"Nurse, take this boy to get some supplies for the troops," said Dr. Ussher in English, and the nurse led me away to a storage room where medical supplies were being kept.

I was given a box of supplies, and then led toward the exit of the hospital with Shant. As I walked past Fimi's bed again, I looked back to see Raffi stare at me. That was the last glimpse I would get of him before leaving. And then I was led toward the front of the building.

"I'll show you the way to the tents, but I cannot stay long," said Shant, taking the rifle from off his back and carrying it, "Just keep up with me, Vartan. I know that you can do this."

Carrying the box with me, I hurried to keep up with Shant as he led me down the empty, winding roads of Aigestan. The air was filled with the sounds of distant gunshots. The marching band wasn't playing at the moment, leaving the moments between the gun shots silent and eerie in the dim, waning daylight. The two of us had to navigate across the town to reach the wounded soldiers; it was a lucky thing Shant seemed to know his way around. There were a couple times where I could swear I heard footsteps and rustling behind us, however I was in too much of a hurry to look back much. Shant seemed fixated on getting me to the medical tents as quickly and as safely as it was possible. We were heading toward Castle Rock, at the edge of town. Castle Rock was a large massive and rocky hill which rose from an otherwise flat plain, and bordered the northern side of the walled portion of Van. Armenian fighters had been hiding out there for weeks now, shooting down at the Turkish soldiers below them when they got the chance. The tents were alongside one of the walls leading up to the rock, sheltered from gunfire.

I could tell we were getting close to the tents when I heard groans of misery coming from wounded soldiers. The tents were big enough for four cots each, and each had an Armenian medic in charge of them, none of them affiliated with foreign relief groups. Near the entrance of each tent were tables with bloodied rags and medical implements on the top.

"Here we are," said Shant, "Your people appreciate the help, Vartan. As soon as you're done, someone will escort you back to the hospital."

A man put his hand on Shant's shoulder, and he turned around.

"Shant, good of you to make it," said the man, "There was a gun fight. Another one of our men was hit in the leg, and he can't walk. "

"The boy here can help you bring him to the tents," said Shant.

"We're short on men up there. We could use your help."

"I was told to return to the hospital," Shant said, "I was only here to escort this boy."

"We've three injured men in the tents, and one more up there. They can handle themselves at Ussher's hospital."

Shant hesitated for a few moments, but then gave a nod, "I will be right up there."

I could sense that Shant was a little bit scared to be going up to fight. I suppose I would have been too. It was frightening enough just going up there to help out. One of the doctors the approached me.

"Ah, you've come with the supplies. Just in time." he said, taking the box from me.

The solider who'd been speaking to Shant now looked to me, "Come on then, boy, help me get the injured down to the tent."

"Follow our lead, Vartan," said Shant.

I obediently complied, and we walked up in a single file line, climbing up the rocky outcropping.

"Be careful now, Vartan... and be brave," Shant warned.

I nodded in response. I had to follow his every move. Soon enough, we came upon the soldiers. There were men dressed in uniforms and fur caps crouched behind rocks with their rifles and pistols aimed downward. I could see the encampment of Turkish soldiers just beyond the walls, some distance away. The sight sent chills down my spine. I felt far too young to be there at that moment. Shant took me to the wounded Armenian soldier. He'd been shot not only in the leg, but also in the right side of his chest. It was worse than we'd thought.

"We need to bring him down carefully," said Shant, "I may as well help you; we don't want to aggravate his injuries any further.

The man groaned as Shant lifted him by the shoulders. Blood streamed from the corner of his mouth. I wondered if this man was going to die. I hoped it wouldn't be because of anything I had done wrong.

"You grab his legs," Shant said.

I obeyed, and carefully we tried to make it down the rock carrying the wounded man. I walked forward with each of the man's legs under my arms, trying to keep low and out of sight of the soldiers down below, knowing that, at any moment, one wrong move could-

There was the sound of a single gunshot. I couldn't be sure where it had come from, which side had shot it. Maybe someone pulled the trigger accidentally. Maybe not. Bullets from the Turkish army began to pepper Castle Rock. I saw Shant's head jerk back, and he fell backwards. I shrieked, as the man we were carrying fell with him with a pained grunt.

"Get down, boy!" the man I had been helping to carry managed to yell at me, and I ducked behind the boulders as bullets sprayed the rocks behind me, making the tiny pebbles hit my skin.

I crawled to Shant, who wasn't moving. Tears were streaming down my cheeks. Blood poured from his skull. Shant was dead. On the ground beside his body was his rifle. Fighting back my tears, I reached for it. I felt in my heart that St. Vartan Mamikonian was watching over me, guiding my hand to defend my people just as he had defended against the Persians. Without really thinking, and having never even shot a real firearm before, I crawled toward a boulder, and rested the barrel of the rifle on top of it. I trembled, holding the rifle up and closing one eye, remembering Shant's lessons with the replica rifles, aiming at the Turkish soldiers who were now bombarding us with bullets. The rifle was loaded, but I wouldn't know how to reload it if I had tried, even if I had known where Shant kept his other bullets. It was quite possible given the shortages that he had no other bullets.

Taking a breath, I squeezed the trigger and shot downwards at the ones who had killed my mentor and protector. There was only one bullet in the rifle. Wanting to make it count, I had aimed for the soldiers in the trenches, my hands trembling and the force of the gun nearly causing me to hit myself in the face. I may never know for sure if I managed to hit anyone, since I was not the only one shooting from the Armenian side. I hoped that whatever makeshift bullet inside that rifle was not wasted. I squeezed the trigger again and again, as if expecting the gun to be filled with infinite ammunition, but nothing happened. It needed bullets and gun powder. After finally giving up at this, I put the rifle down, ducked behind the stone, and began to weep.

"Go back down to the tents," the injured man shouted to me as best he could over the noise, "Someone else will bring me down there. And don't make yourself obvious anymore."

I decided to heed him, though I felt bad for having failed to bring him down to the tents. Perhaps his injury wasn't too fatal, I could not tell. So, crawling on my hands and knees, not daring raise my head up lest I end up like Shant, I slowly made my way back down the rock.

A well-aimed cannon blast exploded at the bottom of Castle Rock, dangerously close to where the medical tents were situated. I was showered with rocks, and enveloped by dust and smoke. I used this smoke as a cloak, getting down the path more quickly, running.

As I made my way down to the bottom I nearly tripped over something lying in my path, a dark shape. After catching my footing I turned around to see what it was, perhaps against my better judgment. I heard a small whimper. At first I thought it was an injured animal. As I kneeled down, it became more and more obvious that it was a human; a child.

"Oh God…"

The child was curled up on the ground, covered in wounds from flying rocks. When I turned him over, his white shirt was covered with a dark stain, glistening in the setting sunlight as the dust began to dissipate. It was a deep wound, perhaps from shrapnel, or even a bullet. I looked at his face. Surely I was hallucinating. Surely, this was not who I thought I was holding in my arms. My heart went cold.

He followed me…why did he follow me…

"Raffi, speak to me!"

Raffi coughed, and looked up at me. He was still alive.

"Vartan...I...I am sorry..." was all he could muster, his voice pitifully feeble.

"Idiot! What were you thinking?! You were supposed to stay at the hospital and wait for me! I need to get you out of here!"

"I wanted...to be brave...to be with you."

I picked him up in my arms, and ran the rest of the way down Castle Rock, towards the hospital tents, as fast as my legs could take me, no longer making an effort to hide myself. I am lucky I didn't end up being shot myself, but nothing else seemed to matter but getting Raffi to the tents. The sound of gunshots and cannons pierced the air. They had taken everything else from me. They were taking everything from my people. I could not bear to have the one thing I had left robbed from me as well.

St. Vartan

I stayed by Raffi's side when the medics at the tent took him in, working frantically to save his life. The area had been disheveled by the canon blast, Raffi wasn't the only one injured by it. Someone else was sent to retrieve the man I was supposed to be transporting, and Shant, who of course died instantly. They tried to dislodge the bullet in Raffi before dealing with his other injuries. It had hit him in the middle of his chest, missing the heart and therefore not killing him. I held his hand as he screamed, cried and bled out. Mercifully, the pain eventually made him lose consciousness. There was talk of moving him to the American hospital, but it was too risky. He could be injured further, or there could be another explosion. It wasn't safe to walk the streets even if it you were uninjured and able to walk on two feet.

While they eventually did shoo me out of the tent so they could work undistracted, I stayed near the tent the whole time. After excruciating hours, I was told by a medic that although they were able to fish the bullet out of him, the damage had been done. Raffi had lost a lot of blood. There was internal damage. But maybe there was a small chance he could make it, if only there were enough medical supplies to go around. But there weren't. It would take liberation by the Russians for more supplies to be brought into Van. In the meantime, I was left to stare at my little brother's mangled body, and wonder why he had followed me. Maybe I had babied him too much, let him depend on me too much. Maybe it was my fault he followed me. Yet he said he wanted to be brave? Was it I who had put that idea in his mind? If I could speak to Fimi I could ask her what made him follow me. But I couldn't leave his side. I wouldn't. Even when some of the soldiers suggested I get back to my Boy Scout troop, I wouldn't budge. Nothing would make me leave Raffi.

That night, one of the fighters approached me. He was tall, with a prominent mustache, dressed in fedayi attire with a rifle strapped to his back. He sat down beside Raffi's cot. By this time I had been allowed back in the tent.

"Sorry about what happened up there," the man said.

I stayed silent, staring at the ground, brooding.

"No one saw that kid follow you guys. That boy must be a stealthy one."

I listened to Raffi's strained breathing. The man's words barely registered, but I heard them.

"Any idea why he followed you? You must care about him a great deal to refuse to go back to the American hospital where it's safe. What is this boy's relationship to you? A close friend? A brother, perhaps?"

I exhaled, looking over to the man.

"He's my brother," I answered.

"Your brother," the man repeated, "And you two are from Sporri's orphanage, are you not? He must be the only family you have left."

"My mother is dead. My father is in the army."

"The Ottoman army?"

"Yes."

The man sighed and shook his head. He was sure my father was dead. And, try as I might to deny it, I knew he was probably right. But mercifully, he chose not to argue the point with me.

"I'm sorry all of this had to happen to you, boy. It's the young who suffer the most in war."

"I know."

"So your little brother just didn't want to be left alone while you came here to help out?"

"I suppose that explains it," I answered simply.

Just when I had thought Raffi was beginning to become more independent too. Maybe he wasn't ready for me to leave someplace so far away from him yet. Maybe I should have said no to Shant. Maybe Shant would be alive if I had stayed at the hospital. The what-ifs plagued me. Plague me. Shant was dead, Raffi looked to be heading the same way, and it was all my fault.

"Some of the other men saw what you did after Shant died. You took up arms in his place, took the fight to the Turks. That took some courage, even if you didn't hit anyone."

I didn't know why I had done it. Courage or momentary insanity, it was either or. But I said nothing. I wanted this man to leave me alone.

"What's your name, son?" he asked me.

"My name is Vartan."

"Vartan. That's a hero's name. Surely you know the story of Vartan Mamikonian, right?"

I scoffed. Of course I did. I was sick of it.

"Everyone knows that one," he said, judging my reaction as a yes, "My name is Aram. Pleasure to meet your acquaintance, Vartan."

I gave a nod.

"You seem like the kind of young man I was once. I think you'll live up to your name. Maybe this siege is your chance to do that."

"I don't see how," I replied, "I got Shant killed, and maybe my little brother too. I should go work with the girls sewing uniforms. Or would I fail at that too?"

"Do not punish yourself so," Aram said, "I was going to suggest one way for you to redeem yourself."

"I cannot leave Raffi's side," I insisted, "Not again."

"There are better ways to help Raffi. To help all of the other sick and injured in this city."

"Yes? And what are they?" I asked, seething with skepticism.

"Allow me to explain our situation to you," Aram said, "Our stores of flour, poultry and meat are pitifully low. The people have taken to eating cats, dogs and donkeys, as you probably well know. Next will be rats. The water in our wells is being polluted by the Turks, who throw piles of the bodies of dead Armenians into the wells outside Aigestan. The American Hospital doesn't have an endless supply of medical tools either, and they can't be replenished as long as the city is under siege. Our soldiers keep getting injured and killed, while Jevdet Bey fills our city with the victims of his minions, who are raping and torturing Armenians across the countryside. Our city cannot withstand this onslaught forever, though we will never outright surrender. One more day of freedom is worth more than that."

I listened. I had thought about how much longer this siege could afford to go on. It didn't seem like it could go on for much longer.

"The only ones who can save us now are the Russians. They have Armenians in their ranks, you know. They would rush to our aid in haste if they only knew what was happening here. But we've only one way of getting word to them."

I began to understand what Aram was about to ask me to do.

"We have sent couriers out to them; people with letters hidden in their clothing. But no word yet on if they made it. These couriers are our city's only hope. It will take a brave soul to volunteer to deliver this message, and give information on our condition to the necessary quarters."

"You wish for me to do this?"

"You have a fire burning inside you, boy. I can see that. You're a natural, born hero. I think you'd be a fine candidate. If you were to reach the Russians, you would be saving your little brother, and your friends at the orphanage, not to mention all of us in Aigestan. We'll try all that we can to save your brother, but we can't give Raffi the proper medical attention he needs until the siege ends."

I stayed silent. Considering what could easily be a suicide mission.

"I would never force you into such an undertaking. But, you can either stay here by your little brother's side and do nothing more or you can take matters into your own hands. What say you?"

I searched my soul for the right answer. I may have been somewhat ignorant of what the world was like outside the walls of our city, but I knew it wasn't good. I had seen the starved and mutilated people streaming into the city each day. I could only imagine what they would do if they captured me and knew I was carrying a message to the Russians. But Aram made a strong argument. It would do Raffi no good for me to simply sit at his side and watch him slowly die. Aid from the Russians could be his only salvation. I had to try. I had to.

A Stab in the Dark

With Raffi's very life on the line, later that night I listened intently to the plans being made around me by the soldiers in charge. A letter would be sewn into the inside of my jacket, hidden on my person. Only I was to know where it was, and if captured, I was under no circumstances to divulge its whereabouts. Though they would probably find it anyway, I thought. My food for the long journey would in the form of thin lavash bread that was to be hidden by way of wrapping it around my belly underneath my shirt. I was also given a canteen of water, which I wore on a strap around my shoulder.

In one tent the soldiers had a map laid out on a wooden table showing the area of the eastern Ottoman Empire, or Western Armenia. Marked on it were rumored positions of invading Russian army units. It was thought they would be invading from the northeast, through Erzurum toward the north of Lake Van, where it was less mountainous. It gradually became apparent that I had been talking to none other than Aram Manukyan, leader of the resistance. No relation to me.

"Needless to say this is going to be a long journey," Aram explained, marking the map with a pencil, "You'll be heading north to northeast, all the way. For navigational purposes, this means you will be keeping Lake Van to your left as you travel. You will have to make your way up past the lake, continuing north as you go, as quickly as your legs can take you. It may take you two or three days to get to the spot, if you are lucky. I suggest that you follow the roads, but not too closely, as they will be monitored. There isn't much cover in the plains outside of the city walls, but beyond that you should stick to wherever there is foliage or rocks. Never lose sight of the road. Travel more by night than by day. We will give you a compass and a lantern, but it would be safest not to use the lantern unless you really get lost. If you see anyone who even looks like they might be a Turk or a Kurd, you hide. It would probably be best to say that if they are anything besides a group of soldiers flying a Russian flag, you hide. Do you understand this, Vartan?"

"Yes, sir," I said, standing stiff, out of respect.

"Good. I want you to make sure your message gets to General Yudenich. He is the Russian general in charge of the Caucasus campaign, and might lend us a hand in pushing back the Turks. If you find the Russians, ask that your message be taken to General Yudenich. May God be with you on your journey. Prepare yourself then, soldier. We will get you your food, and the letter is being sewn into your coat as we speak. In about an hour, a group of men are going to escort you to Tabriz gate. We'll be sending dogs with lanterns tied around their necks out of the other gates as a decoy for the Ottomans to shoot at, but you'll have to make your escape in the dark. Are you ready for this?"

"I am, sir," I replied, my voice slightly shaky, because I didn't know if I was ready.

"I'm sure your brother would be proud," said Aram, putting his hand on my shoulder, "To aid in your mission, I'll give you this."

Aram presented me with a small compass. It was like the one Neville had. He had taught us how to use compasses, but there was never enough for us all to have them, so it had been passed around.

"Oh, and I have one more thing for you."

Aram reached into his pocket, and produced a single bullet. It was very small, and round, looking like it was made for a rifle. He put it into my hand, and closed my fist around it.

"The medic took this out of your little brother. Normally we would use it for our own guns, but I want you to have it. I want you to remember what you're doing this for."

I opened my hand and stared at the bullet that had severely injured Raffi. Such a tiny thing it was. Frowning, I closed my fist around it again. It could very well have been some other bullet, but it was a symbol that motivated me. And Aram knew that it would motivate me. I wasn't going to let Raffi down. I had to go through with this. I had to find the Russian army, and save not only Raffi, but the city.

"There's that fire," Aram said, patting my back, "Now, you are a man. Come, let's get your food, and your jacket."

When we walked out, an old lady in a headscarf approached me with sheets of lavash bread. They had me remove my shirt and lift my arms, and she wrapped the bread around my midsection, giving me around four layers around my thin frame, before putting the shirt over it and tucking it into my pants. Four layers were not as much as one might think; not with how skinny I was. Then I was given the jacket. They were able to find a patch that matched its black color, and I could feel paper inside. Another soldier gave me a lantern, and I was reminded again not to light it unless I absolutely needed to.

Thus, the preparations were complete; two armed soldiers walked with me to Tabriz Gate in the dark of the night. It was just as it had been the night Zangi was killed; covered by armed soldiers on the roofs, lined with destroyed, burned-out buildings, and reeking of death, because it was too dangerous to remove all of the dead bodies. Was I to be the next Zangi?

"When you get out there, you run," said one of the soldiers to me, "Don't even look back. Get around the trenches out there, don't let any Turkish soldier see or hear you. You will have to get around the walls of the city and turn north. There won't be enough light to see your compass, but just try to find the outline of the mountains out there. In general, if you keep the mountains to your right, and the lake to your left, you will be traveling north, that is until you get far enough north to where the lake is north of your position, which is when you will know that it is time to turn to the northeast."

"Understood," I replied.

We waited, crouched behind the same wall we had before. The night was unseasonably cold. But perhaps it was just me. I had felt cold since I found Raffi. All was quiet. The silence only made me more afraid.

"Wait for it..." said the soldier, eyeing a pocket watch with his lantern on, "We're releasing the dogs at half past four, you are to escape through the gate ten minutes before that."

I waited silently. I wondered if this were the end.

"Alight. Go! Run!"

This was it. As if fleeing into the very jaws of Hell, I ran toward Tabriz Gate in the darkness. I had only the moon and the stars to guide me. When I reached the gate, I briefly stopped and looked out at the vastness of the landscape before me, opening out to the east in the direction of Persia. The mountains were a distance away, black jagged shadows against the stars. After gaining enough distance from the city I would keep them to my right. Looking at everything on a map was one thing, but actually having to walk the length of the lake and toward Erzurum? It seemed an impossible task. Lake Van was no small lake.

Trying to remain stealthy, I quickly fled in the direction I knew was east, so that I could turn north when it was safe enough for me to do so. I tried my best to remember where on the map the trenches would be, so I could stay away from them. Running through the grass, I stayed close to the wall, avoiding the road at this point, until finally departing from the safety of the wall and running into the open field. I thought I could make out the trenches and tents of the Ottoman army, and I avoided them.

Within a few minutes, I could hear shooting in the distance. The soldiers had released the dogs from the other gates. The army nearest to me opened fire as well, upon hearing the more distant armies do so. But the sounds were all behind me. They couldn't see me. The Ottoman soldiers didn't know that the messenger had already escaped. But now, I could only use the mountains to navigate, until there was enough light in the sky for me to look at my compass. All I knew was that I was to follow the roads north. I didn't know exactly where the Russians would be, and I don't think that anybody in Van knew for certain either. My mission was one of chance; a stab in the dark.

All I remember of the remainder of that night was running, running nonstop in the darkness, like a frightened rabbit, too afraid of what might happen if I stopped. But it was just before dawn, and the late spring sun was only two hours away from rising. The dangers I faced on this journey would only rise with it. But it marked the direction I needed to be traveling, as I made my way toward where the sky brightened. Gradually it became easier to see my surroundings. I would have to find a road again, having run aimlessly, with only a few breaks in between to rest and catch my breath, just to put as much distance between me and the armies that were besieging the city.

What would my father think of his son now? Was there really any hope now that he would find me in Van and take me home, adopting Raffi too? I had all but given up on that fantasy. Agreeing to this suicide mission was my final act of letting go of hope, in many ways.

Once the sun began to peer over the jagged mountains, I decided it best that I make myself scarce. The land was sparsely populated beyond the city, and for the most part empty. Eventually I found a rocky, wooded area, and crawled behind a boulder as the sun rose. This was to be my shelter; I hadn't slept the whole night, and I'd had nothing to eat since lunch the day before. But I had to ration what little I had. I reached into my shirt and tore off a piece of lavash bread half as wide as my chest, and had a little bit of water from my canteen. With any luck maybe I would find some food or water along the way; but I remembered the look of those half-starved Armenians coming into the city after being marched fifty miles or more. I did have more freedom to look for food and water than they'd had while being forcefully escorted by armed Turkish soldiers, but I knew it was going to be difficult either way. For now, I curled up under the rock, and napped for some time, only hoping not to be discovered as I slept.

When I awoke, the sun was high in the sky. It was still not safe to walk out in the open, but I now had the chance to scout around, and perhaps find a road, if only from a distance. As I walked through the knee-high grass, the sounds of birds replacing the sounds of guns and explosions that had rung in my ears for two weeks. I could almost forget that there was a war going on, and a wholesale slaughter of my people along with. I pulled the compass out of my pocket and followed the wobbly needle. The lake was a blue stripe to my left. The mountains towered to my right. Eventually in the distance, I could see what I thought was a road, or a river. One of the two. I decided I would travel parallel to it, and see where it would take me. As long as it was going north, it would get me somewhere toward where I wanted to get to; the Russians.

The Road

I scarcely remember every detail of my mad dash across the rolling hills and plains of the countryside, though I can remember certain things. I remember at one point seeing a cloud of smoke climbing into the sky from a distance as I reached the tops of the hills. I wondered if perhaps it was a battle sight between the Turks and the Russians; but in reality, by May 4th the Russians hadn't advanced this far south yet. As I got closer, however, I found something far worse. It looked to have been a village once. But it was burned to the ground, save any buildings made of stone. Dead bodies littered the streets and the outside of the village. I got low in the grass, not wanting to be spotted by the marauders who had destroyed this village. It was better to keep my distance. I kept moving on my hands and knees for a long while, and fortunately, got past the village without being seen and mistaken for someone they had forgotten to kill.

I very slowly made my way around the rocky outcroppings which surrounded the valley that Lake Van sat in, keeping to the hills. Remembering Aram's advice to travel more by night, whenever I found a suitable hiding place I would stay there for a while and rest. I was waiting for nightfall for the chance to really make some good distance. That night I pushed forward, fueled by a day of short naps, stopping seldom, only to eat a little bit of bread or relieve myself. I knew better than to stop at the towns and villages I saw along the way. Any that had been mostly Armenian had been looted or destroyed. Many lied abandoned. The only people left there were Turks and Kurds, who had been threatened with death if caught harboring Armenians fleeing the mass killings. But the area was relatively sparsely populated to begin with, and my journey for the first full day was largely uneventful.

On my second day on the road, I encountered a firsthand sight of what was befalling the Armenians in those dark days. While following the road for some distance at around sunset, ahead of me I saw a large group of people traveling down the same road. A few were on horseback, but most were on foot, in single file. I thought at first perhaps they were refugees escaping a destroyed village. I was probably partly right; crouching in the grass, I stayed in place as they walked closer toward me. I couldn't be sure if these people were friendly or not, after all. But soon, I saw this group for what it truly was.

The men on horseback had rifles on their backs, and wore military uniforms and a fez on their heads. Turkish gendarmes. Everyone on foot was a woman, from the looks of their clothing. Not a man to be seen among them. I realized these were Armenians, probably being led to Van to help starve the city out; or elsewhere. There had been rumors abound back in Van about Armenians being marched out into the scalding deserts of Syria, to be killed or left for dead. If true, they really were not going to stop the senseless slaughter until they killed every Armenian in the whole Ottoman Empire. For the moment, I relished in the miracle that I had not been captured and killed yet.

I stayed completely still as this caravan of captives marched down the road, coming from who knows where, whether having marched near or far God alone knows. Once they passed me by, I saw one woman in the line fall to her knees, evidently too exhausted to go on. A gendarme rode over to her, and got off of his horse. After a brief exchange of words, I saw him draw out his scimitar. There were shrieks as he swung down at her. He had a rifle, but maybe he didn't want to waste the bullet. Wiping the blood off on the victim, he sheathed his weapon, and got back on his horse. The caravan moved on. I sat crouched in the grass staring in their direction for some time, until it started to become too dark to see very far, wondering if I should go over and see if the woman was still alive. The victim was probably dead, and if not there wasn't anything I could do for her, but I still felt guilty about leaving. In the end, I had no other choice. She would not be the last bloody, decaying, nameless, corpse I would see alongside the road on my journey, nor was she the first. There were many, discarded like trash, littering the countryside.

By the end of the night Lake Van lay ahead of me, its waters reflecting the moonlight. It was time to turn northeast, after two days of travel. By this time my rations were becoming low. The bread was salty with my sweat, and I disliked eating it. Here and there I would try to find other things I could eat. I tried grass, leaves, flowers, many things. Nothing that was good though. My canteen was low as well. I tried only taking a single sip every time I stopped for bread, to make it last. But the days in May were hot around Lake Van, though the nights were chillingly cold. I would keep myself warm by running.

Another day and night passed. I was losing track of the days. This was the last day of my bread. The situation was becoming desperate. If I did not find the Russians and soon, I was going to starve, and so would Van. I had no way of knowing if the Turks had finally overtaken the city while I was away. But I tried not to burden my mind with such worries. I had one purpose and one purpose alone; to notify the Russians of the siege. After following the lake traveling northeast for a day, napping most of the morning and afternoon behind a tree before proceeding in the early evening, finally I came upon a welcome sight, though I couldn't know that at first glance.

In the distance I could see troops making a hasty retreat down the road. For fear of being seen, I hid behind a rock and watched from a distance. They were Turkish troops. In the distance, a cloud of smoke arose from the ground. The troops were moving with haste, cavalries of men on horseback, some pulling cannons behind them, and many soldiers moving on foot. There were maybe two hundred soldiers in all, not a whole lot relatively speaking. Had they just finished annihilating another village, and were on to the next one? Or were they running from something? After hiding for perhaps two hours, waiting until I could hear the marching no more, I proceeded toward the sight of the battle.

As it turned out, this was the town of Ardjish, a town in the north of the Van province, and the sight of a clash between the Russians and the Ottoman army that had just ended with an Ottoman retreat. When I finally reached this city, many of the buildings were smoldering. But at long last, I could see my salvation. Stationed outside the town in tents with Russian flags were the 2nd Transbaikal Cossack Brigade, and the Araratian Volunteer Brigade; which was comprised of Armenian volunteers from the Russian side of the border in the Caucasus, what is the Armenian SSR today. Word of what the Turks had been doing to the Armenians in the Ottoman Empire had reached at least that far.

As I ran toward the tents, waving my hands, a few soldiers noticed me, and raised their rifles at me.

"Do not shoot! I come from Van!" I shouted.

They did not lower their guns, but they did not shoot either. Some of the soldiers spoke to each other, and as I closed in on their tents, finally they lowered their guns. A soldier shouted something at me in Russian, but I couldn't understand. I tried to tell them I was Armenian. The soldiers spoke to one another, and called someone from the other brigade to the tent. He was a tall, regal man, with curly black hair and a mustache.

"What is it you are trying to tell us, son?" he asked.

"I come from Van," I pleaded, "I've a message for General Yudenich of the Russian army. We have been under siege for more than two weeks, and we need your help."

"Remove your coat," he said, and I complied. He handed it to some other soldiers, who would cut open the patch. They apparently were aware that the message would be hidden in my clothes.

"You can call me General Vartan," the man said, "You look like you've been starving. How long did it take you to get here from Van?"

"Maybe four days," I replied, interested in the fact that he was another Vartan, "I've lost track. It has been a hard journey; I am almost completely out of food and water."

"Provisions in this town probably aren't much better than Van, but we'll get you fed with something, the army has its supplies," the general said, "Come along to my tent."

I followed him, feeling a little cold without my jacket as night began to fall. I was looking like a skeleton with my ribs showing through my shirt, having been in a state of mild starvation even before leaving Van.

"What's your name, boy?" the General asked.

"Vartan Manukyan," I replied.

He chuckled a bit and opened the flap to his tent, "Vartan? Is it your birth name?"

"Yes, sir."

There were seats in his tent, and a table with a map laid out. The map had several pins sticking out of it.

"I have a lot of respect for you, making it all this way. I respect you enough to let you in on something. General Vartan is my war name. My real name is Sargis Mehrabyan."

I nodded.

"Don't let me hear you call me that in front of the other men though," he warned.

Another Armenian soldier entered the tent, with my letter in his hand. He gave it to Sargis.

"Here it is," he said, taking it and reading it, "You aren't the first courier to make it through, as there've been some eleven others, but you are the most recent. This will be a good update on how our brothers in Van are faring. We are on our way to Van now in fact, on General Yudenich's orders. We leave in the morning to advance south along Lake Van; you are welcome to join us. You will have made your family proud on your return, having taken on such a heroic task."

"I'm an orphan, sir," I said.

"Oh? I am sorry to hear that. Was it the Turks?"

"Not with my mother and sister, they died of sickness some years ago…but perhaps with my father. He was drafted into the army…"

Sargis nodded knowingly, aware of what must have happened, "Then you've already made them proud, from heaven. You know the old saying, don't you? Van in this world, paradise in the next. That is where your family is now."

That was a saying that got passed around in Van a lot, rumored to be centuries old.

"Go and get yourself fed and rested," Sargis said, "I need to plan our route, and prepare to free this land from Jevdet the Butcher. We leave at dawn, if you are willing, you may follow us, and help out the soldiers.

So, after thanking General Vartan, I exited the tent. Several soldiers were sitting around a campfire outside and roasting some meat, and they invited me over to sit with them, having already heard that I was a messenger from Van who had made it here on foot. They had forced the Turks to retreat today. The remaining Armenian population in Ardjish was safe, but the Turkish and Kurdish population had evacuated before hostilities began. The soldiers were understandably tired and hungry; after some food and rest they said they would make haste to save the people of Van. I hoped the city could wait one more night, but I supposed an army marches on its stomach. They stood a much better chance of matching the Ottoman Turkish army's might if rested.

Liberation

The next morning, the army moved out, advancing down the road to the next target, leaving some men behind to defend the city if the Ottomans tried to make a rebound. But the Ottoman Empire was failing when it came to the Caucasus campaign against Russia, choosing to put more of its focus elsewhere, and Jevdet Bey's forces were putting up a very weak fight. When finally the 2nd Transbaikal Cossack Brigade and the Araratian Volunteer Brigade arrived to the city of Van on May the 17th, Jevdet's army and all of the Muslim citizens of the other quarters of the city had already evacuated the night before, upon hearing of the Russian advance. But to cover up their retreat, the Turkish army had bombed the city heavily and indiscriminately. Clouds of smoke rose up behind the walls when we rode towards Van. Houses, churches, and other buildings in Aigestan had been completely destroyed.

The brigades were welcomed with cheers, the marching band played with victorious pride, and though the city was in partial ruin and the bodies of the dead littered the streets, there was rejoicing. I split off from the brigade soon after entering Tabriz gate, and made my way for the American Mission Hospital. I quickly navigated the twisted streets, unfazed by the death and destruction around me. I remembered this route, the same route Raffi and I had taken when we were delivering that dog to the soldier. The only difference was the level of destruction, the number of mangled, charred bodies in the road.

When I turned down the street that the hospital was on, what I found was a gruesome discovery; the whole front of the hospital was gone, the rest of the building crumbling. Blackened with soot, smoke wafting from the rubble. It appeared the Ottomans had finally targeted American territory. Would it be enough to draw them into the war? It was anybody's guess at the time whether this egregious breach of diplomacy would be enough to do that; but evidently, America's entry into the Great War still didn't happen for two more years. More urgently to me, I still had no idea where Raffi was.

I headed for the orphanage next. If anyone I knew survived the bombing, they would probably be there. I wondered though if my fellow Boy Scouts had been released from their service yet now that the Russians had liberated us. I made haste, down the ruined streets, the victorious sound of Van's marching band filling the air. Everyone celebrating but me.

Eventually, I returned to the gray, war torn building that housed Herr Sporri's orphanage. Windows were boarded up due to being broken, but it was fairly intact. When I entered through the double doors, I was immediately recognized by Siran the nursemaid.

"Vartan? You're alive!" she said, rushing over to hug me as other children stared in my direction. This was somewhat strange to me, as Siran had never showed me any affection before. Maybe it was the siege that had changed her. "Come, I'll bring you to Herr Sporri. You look half-starved."

I followed, hoping desperately to find Raffi here. Many of the orphans were still out, the nursemaids had taken them into the streets to revel in the celebrations. The only ones still here were injured or very young. Herr Sporri's office looked the same as ever when we entered it. Untouched by the destruction. It was strange being back in familiar surroundings.

"Another of the missing boys has returned," said Siran.

"Mr. Manukyan," said Herr Sporri, looking at me over his desk "If my eyes don't deceive me."

"Herr Sporri," I began, "The hospital, it's been destroyed."

"Bombed during the Ottoman army's retreat," Herr Sporri explained, "Fortunately it had been completely evacuated beforehand. Not everyplace was so fortunate. What is unfortunate is how many of our boys went missing during the siege, and how many more orphans we now have to house after the siege."

"Is Raffi here?" I asked immediately.

"Raffi...Maghazadjian? Your friend, correct?"

I nodded.

"He went missing at the same time you did. I regret to say I know nothing of his whereabouts from the time you two were working at the hospital."

"He was at the medical tents of the soldiers," I explained, fearing the worst if he was not at the orphanage, "He'd been shot. He followed me when I was chosen to help Shant at Castle Rock."

Herr Sporri wore a solemn expression, "He should not have been there. I'm sorry, but I don't know what became of him. I can ask Dr. Ussher if he knows more. You and him were only two of several of our orphans that had gone missing."

"And the dead?" I asked.

"Regrettably, at least six deaths that I know of. Raffi may still be alive somewhere for all we know, in the coming days I'm sure we'll find more of the missing. May I ask where you have been?"

"Aram Manukyan sent me out of the city to deliver a message to the Russians."

Both Siran and Herr Sporri were struck silent for a moment.

"You are the first I've heard of that returned from such a mission," said Herr Sporri, "Well done."

"That would explain why he looks so famished," said Siran, "Come along to the dining hall, it is almost lunch."

"You'll find that the food supply will improve in the coming days," Herr Sporri added, "For as long as the Russians are able to keep the city, at least."

Siran led me out of the office, and back toward the dining hall. More of the orphans had returned indoors now. The orphanage was filled to capacity now, and more crowded than it had ever been. Sporri's orphanage was one of the smaller ones in Van, one could only imagine what the Reynold's orphanage looked like right now. Searching the benches for a familiar face, finally I came to see Fimi sitting among a group of girls. Our eyes connected, and she looked at me with shock.

"Vartan!" she called out, getting up out of her seat, still wearing a sling on her arm.

I walked over to her, and she forced the girl next to her to scoot to the side so that I could sit.

"Where have you been? I thought you and Raffi were dead! Where is Raffi?"

I waited for her questions to pause before interjecting with my answer. I decided to wait to tell her about my journey. There was only one thing I wanted to know from her.

"I don't know where Raffi is now. I was wondering if you knew something. What happened the last time you saw him?"

"Well, it was back at the hospital," she began, "After you were gone, he just got really quiet, watching Dr. Ussher fix me up, looking at the other patients. You remember how horrible it was in there. I don't quite remember when he wandered off, but he was gone by the time Dr. Ussher pulled out everything that was stuck in my skin and put the splint on me."

Her long-sleeved dress and headscarf hid any scars or stitches that might have still been there. I could only wonder what drove Raffi to leave. Maybe being alone with the mutilated, screaming and groaning patients was too much for the boy to stand.

"Raffi's not here, and Herr Sporri doesn't know where Raffi is," I said, not wanting to face the very likely possibility that I wasn't going to find Raffi.

"Did he follow you?" Fimi asked.

I nodded, crestfallen.

"What happened?"

I was silent, letting the loud chatter of the other children fill the gap in our conversation.

"Raffi followed me to Castle Rock. He got hit by a bullet. The soldiers were taking care of him, but…"

Fimi stared at me, shaking her head, "You're…you're making things up."

"I wish this were another of my stories," I replied.

"Raffi's….dead?"

I remained silent. Fimi wrapped her uninjured arm around my shoulder, her body shaking with her soft sobs. My eyes watered, but I didn't break down with her. The pain wasn't fresh anymore. It was beginning to sour, fester, and turn into darkness and bitterness. But, what Fimi had told me was all I would ever know about the last day I saw Raffi.

And there the two of us were, embracing in a crowded lunchroom, none of the other kids paying any attention to us. The only two people who were ever going to mourn the loss of this anonymous orphan boy. The only two who would even remember him now that he was gone.

Maybe Raffi lived somehow, and I just never found him again. Maybe Raffi slipped through the cracks, and he was somewhere else in the city. Or maybe Raffi never made it out of the tents. Maybe the soldiers lied about getting the bullet out just to talk me into risking my life sending a message to the Russians. Maybe he was among the piles of thousands of dead bodies the Russian soldiers cremated outside the city in a mass grave in the aftermath of the siege. Another number. Another statistic. My little brother. Raffi Ma-gha-zad-jian. The one who helped me cope with my early days as an orphan. It is as if he never existed. In the fifteen years since, I've entertained the thought that maybe Raffi never existed; maybe he's a memory my mind constructed in the aftermath, maybe he represents my inner-child, that was killed during the siege. Raffi was a part of me that died and could never be brought back.

The maybes, all of them, plague me to this day.

The Hole

There's light. Light coming through the bars in my window. I lay on my back, my arm hanging lifelessly over the edge of the bed. I open my frosty eyelids for the first time in hours. My skin is pale blue. I can see it on my icy hands as I hold them in front of my face, contemplating them. But it doesn't feel cold anymore. I feel alright. The sun makes me feel happy. I can hear the other prisoners outside, working. Guards yelling. Another day at the Gulag. My absence unnoticed. I can barely breathe through my congested lungs. I no longer care.

"Vartan..."

My eyes roll upward. Toward the door. Toward the sound. Am I imagining things?

"Vartan, are you alive in there?"

It is hard to move. I feel as if my very muscles are frozen. I turn, to look at the door. A face looks at me through the window. It's Krikor. He looks shocked when he sees me. I must be a sight.

"God have mercy on you dear boy," he says.

I remain silent.

"I can't stay long. My absence from the Mess Hall will be noticed. Avedik distracted a guard for me, but he can't keep their attention forever."

I clear my throat.

"What happened after I was put in here?" I ask, my voice straining.

"Viken is still in the infirmary after what you did to him," Krikor answers, "It's just the three of us working on the new barracks today. Our prospects for getting dinner don't look good."

"I apologize."

"There's no need my son. We don't blame you. See, I brought you some bread."

He reaches between the bars, and drops his bread on the floor.

I open my mouth, and force the words out, "Don't do that."

"The guards are trying to starve you out. The disciplinary camps are too crowded. It costs them less money if you die in here. I will share my bread with you each day, so that you may live."

"I'm already dead," I reply, my voice raspy.

"No you aren't," he insists, "Listen; do you remember the story of St. Gregory the Illuminator?"

I can't believe he's bringing this foolish story up to me at a time like this.

"He was imprisoned in a pit full of scorpions and snakes for ten years. But he survived. He survived because he was a saint. The snakes and scorpions wouldn't bite or sting him. And he was fed a loaf of bread every day by the queen, who felt pity for him. And when they took him out of the pit, so that he might cure the pagan

King Trdat, he was healthy and unscathed. He cured the king, and the king became a Christian, as did the whole country of Armenia."

"Are you calling me a saint?" I ask, before coughing again.

"I'm saying you can survive this. Don't let them break you."

"Real life...isn't like the fables and fairy tales we grew up believing."

"Maybe it can be, if you take their lessons to heart, and don't give up."

My chest muscles clench as I start to laugh. It turns into a coughing fit.

"Why are you laughing?" Krikor asked.

I gasp for breath, and try to stave off the coughs.

"You...remind me of a boy I used to know."

A Russian guard yells. Krikor has to leave, or else he could end up in a cell too. The bread remains on the floor. I haven't the strength to get to my feet and pick it up. I can feel my body slipping away. Succumbing. My mind so far gone I'm left wondering if Krikor was ever really there at all.

Evacuation

The peace after the siege was short-lived. Van was a self-governed city state for around two months, and though Neville's Boy Scouts were sometimes deployed for things like rebuilding destroyed structures, we were able to go back to being children again. Not that many of us could go back to being children after what we had lived through. By July, the Ottoman army managed to mount a counter-offensive against the Russians, pushing back into its former territories. Aram Manukyan and General Vartan announced the evacuation on July 18th. What we'd fought and died for was all for naught. The Armenians had to leave for Russian Armenia, on foot, with little defense from bands of Kurdish bandits and mercenaries. It was little better than the death marches the Turkish soldiers were putting Armenians on elsewhere in the empire. It would be close to a month before I made it across a bloody Arax river, filled with the corpses of slain Armenians, to Etchmiadzin.

It was so hot. Day after day, week after week, nothing but walking, walking until my feet were raw and blistered. So thirsty. People collapsing around me of exhaustion and heat stroke. My skin, burned, seared and peeling under the punishing, blazing sun. At least Raffi didn't have to go through that.

I'm so glad I'm cold now...

The orphanages were disbanded, I never knew what happened to Ussher or Sporri but I assume they went back to their countries. As for Fimi, well, I did see her again at the orphanage, but for the brief two months of peace I was distant from everyone. It was after I lost Raffi that my true stay in the odinochka began. She fell out of my life. I regret that. But, we would have been sent to separate orphanages in the end.

I spent the rest of my years at an orphanage in Yerevan. I had an angry adolescence, isolating myself from my peers, wanting to blame the world for what had happened in Van. I would get into fights, not unlike the fight with Viken that landed me here. My anger cooled by my twenties, but I still never really recovered. I don't think anybody else who was there really has. It was from those days on that I became an agnostic of sorts. I wonder if Vartan Mamikonian would slap me for being such a heretic, for doubting the religion he died to defend. But would he do that to someone suffering pneumonia and hypothermia in solitary confinement? I've seen the cruelty of the world, and I can only make sense of it my own way. Should I end up in Hell, well, there's nothing they can do to me down there that hasn't already been done to me up here.

Having no place else to go, I stayed at the orphanage after reaching adulthood, only this time, to teach. I taught history and literature, getting to tell stories to the next generation of orphans. It was something I was good at. The times changed; Armenia's short-lived independence won at Sardarapat was taken away when the Soviets took control. But the day that sealed my fate was the day I joined the Dashnaks. Maybe I shouldn't have listened to the man discreetly handing out pamphlets on the street corner, maybe I shouldn't have attended the secret meetings, only to have my name ratted out by a Soviet spy. But a part of me always did have a death wish. I think, on a subconscious level, I did this to myself on purpose. A long way to go for an assisted suicide I suppose.

It should have been me who died, not Raffi. It should have been my body among that mountain of human bodies the Russians cremated after the siege. Not Raffi's. Now, here in odinochka, I can finally martyr myself like I was always supposed to. Raffi, you little fool…it should have been me.

I feel warm. My eyes have been frozen shut for hours now. In the blackness, I feel only peace. Let the darkness take me now. I am ready.

I feel a hand stroke my face.

"I'm sorry, Vartan."

My lip quivers, as I open it to speak.

"Why did you follow me to Castle Rock?"

"I was scared I wouldn't see you again."

"Well you see how that turned out, fool."

"I know…but we can be together now, can't we?"

"I…suppose so, yes. I missed you, you know."

"Come on, let's get out of here Vartan."

He tugs my arm, pulling me up off of the hard wooden cot.

"This is a Gulag, Raffi. No one leaves, alive anyway."

"Come on, get up. Do you feel cold anymore?"

I feel my sides, and my face. I do feel warm. The air I breathe feels warm. I feel like it is springtime. But not Siberian springtime. Like back home's spring time.

"No, I don't. That's odd…"

"What about your cough?"

I breathe deep. No urge to cough. No congested chest.

"It feels better."

"I knew it would, Vartan. Come on, stand up."

I stand on my own two feet, the pain in my knees from being thrown in the cell gone now. There is no snow blowing through the open barred window. Instead I see beams of sunlight. Even the ice caking the walls is gone.

"Come on, we'll go home and you can tell me some more stories. I bet you know all sorts of new ones now, don't you?"

"You are right about that. I could tell you all of Davit of Sasun now."

I get to my feet, led by this little boy to the door. He opens it. We are not at the camp anymore. The air is clean and warm. It's Lake Van. The trees are blossoming, the skies are clear. It is February I think. Around the time we celebrated St. Vartan at the Sourp Khatch church.

"I haven't been here in fifteen years. It's been too long."

Holding Raffi's hand, we walk along the shore. I don't look back at the door we walked through. If I do I might see odinochka, and realize this is all some fantasy. I don't want to be back in prison, after all. The real world is cold, harsh, evil. No, I look forward. There is no better way to escape prison than this. We're walking back to Van. Everything that was bombed out is built right back up again now. There's no Jevdet Bey. The Turks are our friends here. We'll go back to the orphanage and see Fimi again. My father will be waiting to pick the two of us up at the orphanage and take us home. Maybe he'll take Fimi too, do you think so Raffi?

I open my eyes, staring at the dead, lifeless light bulb above my cot.

Van in this world, paradise in the next, so the old saying goes.

Acknowledgements

I would like to thank all of my teachers (particularly my thesis chairs Alex Espinoza, Randa Jarrar and Barlow Der Mugrdechian), my editor, my creative writing course classmates, my fiancé Deborah who provided the cover painting with her amazing artistic skills, my aunt Sharon for being my first reader, my aunt Satenik for introducing me to the story of my grandfather, and my family without whose help this book would never have been completed.

Thank you for your patience and guidance, your use of the editor's red pen.

And to you, my dear readers, if you enjoyed reading this book, please feel free to leave a review on Amazon.com or Goodreads. Thank you, you deserve a golden apple from heaven.

www.ingramcontent.com/pod-product-compliance
Lightning Source LLC
Chambersburg PA
CBHW021245260626
47155CB00004BA/1342